STILL LIFE

A Collection of Short Stories

Matthew Stramoski

With gratitude to A. B. Bentley for her unfailing patience, gentle encouragement, and loving (yet realistic) support.

It always seems impossible until it is done.

NELSON MANDELA

CONTENTS

MATTHEW STRAMOSKI

THE SHORT REIGN OF ALAN THE FIRST

or

It's My Reign and I'll Parade If I Want To

Alan sat in the restaurant's waiting area on a chair by the window. His hair was beginning to gray, but its natural red was still visible between the narrow, discrete streaks of purple. He wore a tie-dyed tank top and baggy knee-length shorts, yellow with a vivid green serpent sinuously intertwined with a flowering vine. He seemed to be casually, unintentionally displaying his skillfully sculpted arms, and the outline of his prominent pectorals could be seen through the fabric. His slender fingers held upright between his open knees a pair of aluminum crutches. He wore one brown sandal; a dull gray medical boot encased his right leg.

Two couples who looked old enough to have recently retired occupied the seats arcing to his right. They chatted among themselves in pointedly cheerful tones.

A young woman with a boy who was almost old enough for kindergarten entered and spoke to the head waiter. Told it would be a twenty-minute wait, they took the two remaining seats in the waiting area, the boy slouching directly across from the man with the crutches.

The young mother's ample breasts filled the top of a

sleeveless blue cotton blouse, their nipples indenting the air. Her shorts clung to her shapely thighs.

The two retired men attempted a discreet glance in her direction, and the older one succeeded in maintaining the flow of the account of his triumph at the eighteenth hole.

The boy's hands remained in his jean pockets even when he sat. His mother said, "Sit up straight, Jeffrey."

He pulled his hands out of his pockets, folded his arms across his t-shirt, and examined from hair to boot the flamboyance seated across from him.

The mother subtly elbowed the boy, who ignored the jab the first time and returned it the second time. "What?"

The mother whispered, "Don't stare, Jeffrey."

"But please," said Alan. "It is my lifelong aspiration to be admired. The more blatant the stare, the more gratified my ego."

Jeffrey leaned forward and tapped the top of the boot with his index finger. "Wudja do?"

"Jeffrey!" His mother glared, first at her son, then at the stranger.

Alan lifted his boot leg. "A slight error in judgment, Jeff. I trusted my friends."

Jeffrey's mother warned, "Don't pry, Jef*frey*." She stressed the last syllable of her son's name, lifted her nose tip a subtle quarter inch, and frowned a warning toward the stranger.

The stranger asked, "Would you like to hear about it?"

"Sure," Jeffrey said.

"*Jeff*rey," his mother admonished.

Jeffrey tried to sit up, realized he was already straight, and asked, "Did it hurt?'

"Absolutely! Delightfully painful, even to retell it."

The boy leaned forward and clasped his hands, leaning his elbows on his knees.

"There's a big parade every year in June. It's a kind of celebration, a festival you might say. I was determined to be part of the parade, but not lost in some group that didn't reflect who I am. My friends told me I was crazy. I didn't represent anything other than myself, as if that wasn't worth parading. I wasn't going to be stonewalled.

"'Why is it,' I asked my *girl*friends, 'that it's only bars and clubs and political groups that get to strut? Why not something that's truly meaningful? Like a *person!*' Let me tell you, Jeff, there's nothing more real than a person.

"I went down to the committee office and in*sss*isted I be put on the roster, but the thing in charge refused my simple request. I couldn't walk all by myself, although there wasn't anything wrong with my legs or feet at that time. Missy said I'd need more than my fabulosity to make the cut. Can you believe the audacity of the man?"

Jeffrey cocked his head and looked puzzled.

"I can see you're baffled too. I told him, 'That doesn't make any sense.'

"'It doesn't matter,' Miss Bossy said; 'rules are rules.'"

Jeffrey broke in. "That's what my dad says."

"I understand how that makes you feel.

"I refrained from raising my voice although I wanted to slap his silly jowls. 'Even when the rules are stupid?'

"The little pig-nose said, 'Especially when they're stupid.'"

Jeffrey's jaw dropped. "That's what my dad says."

Jeffrey paid no attention when his mother said, "Close your mouth, Jeffrey."

"I could tell you'd understand. Frustrating, even maddening, but what can you do when the one in charge thinks he knows enough to make the rules?" With his mouth closed firmly and turned down at the corners, Alan expelled a noisy gust through his nose.

The maître d' called, "Jensen, party of four." The retired contingent rose and departed in deathly silence.

Alan continued, "The next morning at the gym—" Alan flexed his biceps by lifting his crutches in a curl. "You can see I work out, can't you?"

Without waiting for an answer, he went on, "I told my body buds *all* about the in*dig*nity I had *suff*ered at the hands of that *ig*norant——person. As I said earlier, they were *hard*ly sympathetic. I decided to pull out my —oh I hate to call it that type of card; that word has become *so* —how shall I say— distasteful that it makes me want to spit it out."

Alan shook his shoulders as if chilled by an evil spirit's passing. "Let's just say I insisted they help me with my plan. I proclaimed in my most regal voice, 'You *will all* of you help me. I will go as a queen!'"

"A queen?" Jeffrey looked puzzled. "But you're a man."

Alan said, "It's like Halloween, but it lasts a lifetime. And I thank you for acknowledging my *mas*culinity.

"My body buds postured as usual, showing a pretense of reluctance. But when I challenged them to *prove* they could lift me on my litter, they couldn't help but dare to agree.

"At the committee, I was accepted as leader and ambassador of the Gymnasium Grunters (although none of my buds would be gauche enough to grunt). One quick round of the thrift stores, a visit to a scrumptious budding carpenter, and *voilà!* All was ready.

"Just picture this fabulous scene. My glittering throne perched on a gold-painted litter, the four bearers oiled and clad in Lycra shorts, my fabulous gown, crown, and frown looking down on the crowd. The bearers bowed, grabbed the support shafts, and hoisted me into the air. It went smoother than I expected. All was perfect. They slid the shafts onto their oiled shoulders, and still all was flawless. Then——Fred sneezed."

Jeffrey burst into laughter.

"Yes, Jeff. Down I came. And that is how I got the boot and came to rue the day that I was borne."

Jeffrey's mother groaned.

"Next year," said Alan, "I go as Mildred Pierce."

The maître d' called, "Alana, party of one."

As Alan left, he heard Jeffrey say to his mother, "Mom, he's my new hero. Can we eat with him?"

The mother answered, "Sometimes I worry about you, but I love you just the same."

THE SAINTLY MOTHER

The priest Christopher Charles Kramer was born to Magdalene, unattended, on the winter solstice in the depth and darkness of the season's first severe snow. Her water broke in the night five weeks before term and one hour before dawn.

The midwife lived in town, an eight-mile trek along a narrow trail through the forest and then along a railroad track for another two miles. Although Magdalene did not know that the birth would wait another nine hours, she suspected there was no sense starting for town because there was no way of knowing where along the journey the birth might waylay her.

Magdalene slipped awkwardly from the bed, quietly so as not to awaken her husband. She kindled and stoked the fire in the hearth and added a hard foot of dried fir trunk. She filled the cast iron kettle with water, one pot at a time. She nestled it in the flames then retrieved a stack of rags from the chest at the foot of the bed. When the water began to simmer, she put half of them in the kettle and stirred them with a ladle until they were thoroughly submerged.

Jack Kramer stirred in the bed and his snore changed timbre. She knew that meant he would struggle up in a few minutes, hungry and grumpy.

Half an hour after dawn, Jack came to. He tried not to be angry about the dampness of the thin, sagging mattress, but he often found it difficult, sometimes impossible, to remain unmoved by inconveniences, even those that could not be helped.

Without speaking, he put on his coat and headed to the outhouse.

She cut and fried three thick rashers of bacon and brought a cup of the leftover baked beans to a simmer. She placed a chunk of bread on top of the beans to warm. When she heard her husband coming back, she slopped all of it onto a wooden dish. He hung his coat and took his place at the table.

"My water broke, Jack." She set the dish on the table.

"Yeah."

"Ain't no sense in me goin' for Emma. I'll have to brave it out on my lonesome."

"Huh."

"Yuh c'n do somethin' outside. Kill and pluck the chicken maybe. I might be up for cookin' it this afternoon. Jus' in case I ain't up to fixin' lunch, I put a coupla chunka cheese and some bread in yer haversack with yer bottle, jus' in case yuh wanna take off. But I think y'oughta stay." She prayed she had talked him out of going while hoping she had failed.

Jack chewed a forkful of beans then closed his mouth, his lower jaw offset to the left. His eyelids were half closed.

Magdalene tried to ambush his objection. "No sense arguin'. Ain't nothin' else to eat without me makin' a fuss all day."

"People gonna talk. Gotta go."

"Wha'd'yuh care? People gonna talk even with nothin' to say jus' cuz they can."

He finished his food and pushed his plate to the edge of the table. "I won' be no good an' I won' tolerate no screamin'."

She rescued the plate before he could push it off the table. Before she turned, she asked, "Enough? Wan' more?"

"Whad I wan', you ain't got."

She, silently: Wha' I ain't got, you ain't given. Aloud, from the sink, she said, "Yuh seen the sky? A storm's a-commin'. Ter'ble lookin', too. Best stay near, if yuh can."

Without answering, he geared up for his winter trek. He grabbed the haversack, took the rifle from the rack, banged the door open, and left in agitated silence. She waited until she heard him step off the porch before she crossed from the sink to the door. From the shadows within the house, she watched him disappear into the shallow dimness beneath the pines. She shut the door and for the first time that day allowed herself the luxury of a grimace.

He had not struck her. He had not criticized her but once. He had not forced her. It was a good day.

A t midday, the wind beat the treetops and shook the underbrush, and the hail attacked the forest floor. Within half an hour, the path was lightly covered. Within three hours, the hail had given way to snow. By sundown, the path appeared impassable.

Christopher made his appearance early in the evening, while the winds were at their fiercest. Because he was premature, his mother, trying to be simultaneously optimistic and realistic, predicted that the man would leave late in life if the baby could manage to stay to end of the week.

When he was two days old, Magdalene found the stamina to begin cleaning. Christmas came, but Santa Claus passed over, out of sight, leaving not even a nod; the new mother managed to boil and hang the soiled rags to dry.

On New Year's Eve, Magdalene judged the path passable, if God could be persuaded to help her through the forest. She rose before dawn to feed and swaddle Christopher. She suspended him from her shoulders in a sling, donned as many layers of clothing as she could wrap herself in without hampering her movement, and left the cabin. Intent on her mission, she neither looked back nor noticed that the door was left open.

In the forest, the path began to clear sooner than she had guessed. The days following the storm had been sunny and relatively warm. Intermittent breezes had drifted up from the valley and hastened the snow melt. Only six hours had elapsed between the cabin and the edge of the meadow beside the railroad tracks. She skirted the meadow, preferring the occasional tangle of brush to the sedge and grasses which must surely have been boggy.

Magdalene fortified herself with the thought that her son must be destined for some importance in the Kingdom of Heaven, for why else would the path have been so clear? Certainly, the warm breeze was sent like the winds that opened the Red Sea to aid the passage of his servants. And what of the Pharaoh?

As if summoned by her thoughts, clouds came from the west, covering the horizon. Magdalene repented of her pride in a son who had done nothing yet but live a week.

She stepped cautiously between the rails, not from fear of awakening a sleeper, but from concern that her foot might betray her, find the patch of ice waiting to bring about her fall, and leave her ditched beside the tracks.

Less than a mile from town, the tracks curved to the right around a hill, left the forest to cross a trestle bridge that stretched across a chasm, then bent and hid in a stand of ponderosa pine. Magdalene paused the length of a Hail Mary. She did not see ice on the straight and narrow between the rails. Neither ahead nor behind could she see smoke against the clouds. She listened. She heard only the faint rustle and sighing of the pines.

She stepped forward from rail to rail with her right foot. Her left foot stepped to join it. She stepped forward, looking down only to find the next tie, repeating the Act of Contrition with each step as if telling a rosary.

She wondered if echoing the words of a stranger were enough. In her heart she could not find repentance for marrying Jack. With him, she had produced this son, the first of hers to live.

She was a dozen ties distant from the opposite rim when, through the slot at her feet, she glimpsed a tangle of cloth beside a canvas haversack and glinting shards of glass. She jerked her head up, stood unmoving (for how long she could not say). Her sight blurred, as if a lash had caused her eyes to tear. Before her, she saw a dark arm in the grove beckon unsteadily. As her eyes followed it, she swayed, almost losing her balance. Her shallow breath steadied and deepened, slowly. When she cleared her eyes with the back of her hand, the arm became a shadow, a bowing branch. She waited to feel steady enough to step forward again, more mindful of the gaps than the ties.

Moments after, she heard a whistle warning of a train's approach. Carefully, she quickened her pace. The moment she reached the end of the bridge, she glanced over her shoulder and saw the black engine belch at the far edge of the abyss.

She turned off where the snow was shallow and hid in the grove, unwilling to be seen at that moment and place that she felt were hers alone. But as the freight cars clattered past, the baby cried.

I t was dusk and the evening service had only reached the Offertory when Magdalene sat in the pew farthest from the altar. Emma came and sat beside her. "The baby!" she whispered. "Boy or girl?"

"Boy." He mewled and sought nourishment in the church.

"Jack?"

"I dunno where." It was not for her to decide. She told herself she could not know his heart as well as God, who alone could judge.

After Mass, the child was baptized Christopher Charles Kramer.

MATTHEW STRAMOSKI

BROKEN

Paul's shoe tangled in the wide webbing of the wire fence just as he was leaping to the ground. His body twisted as it descended, and his foot freed itself. He crashed into the grey-brown dust, his arms extended to break the fall. He barely missed landing on the softball he had gone to retrieve. When he rolled onto his back, his left arm extended flat across the ground, the forearm bent near the wrist like a textbook illustration of a fault line.

Marty saw the break but asked reflexively, "Are you OK?"

Paul moaned but did not otherwise answer.

Marty turned and hurried toward the back door of Nanny's house. "Watch him. Don't let him get up."

With the fence between Paul and me, I didn't know how I would prevent him from standing up if he had a mind to.

Mary came over from the back porch with her Raggedy Ann doll clasped in her armpit. She started crying when she reached the fence. "Don't die, Paul."

Marty flew back out of the house and started climbing the fence. The back door of the house slammed. Nanny yelled, "Don't climb!" Marty came back down on the other side.

Nanny stood beside me, hands on her hips, and took a moment to stare at Paul. "Don't go climbing fences, and don't go falling. Look what you've done to yourself." She turned and fretted her way back indoors.

Paul stood up, holding his left wrist in his right hand, trying to steady it, gritting his teeth. He paralleled the fence line toward the street. I ran across the yard, out the gate, and down the driveway. Mary called after me, "Don't let him die, Blaine."

I met my brothers on the sidewalk. Marty said, "We're going to the hospital. Don't nobody get panicky."

Mary caught up with us. Still crying, she offered her doll to Paul. "You can hold Annie. She makes you feel good."

Marty told her to go inside and wait for Mom and Dad. "Tell them we went to the hospital."

We turned right at the first corner and headed for the hospital, although we had no idea where it was. We were headed instead toward Bossier City, the poorer sister to Shreveport, on the wrong side of the tracks. You'd be more likely to find a hospital in the back aisle of a grocery store, but I trusted my older brothers to know.

We had gone almost a quarter mile and had just started up the bridge that arched over the railroad tracks when an unmarked car with a removable flashing bubble pulled up beside us. Marty and I piled in the back seat; Paul sat in front. Without a word, the plainclothes behind the wheel made a U-turn and sped to the hospital, turning his head at the intersections, watching the road ahead, and glancing without comment at Paul. He pulled up to the Emergency Room entrance. Marty got out and opened the door for Paul. The man drove away. He hadn't said a word.

Paul was taken beyond a door. Marty and I sat in the waiting room. A man dressed all in white and carrying a clipboard approached us. "Are you with Paul? Where's his parents?"

Marty answered, "They went shopping. I don't know where."

"Do they have insurance?"

"I don't know."

I said, "It's something blue. A sword, a cross. Something blue."

The waiting room wasn't crowded. A few people sat along

a wall; another group kept to themselves near the back. The entrances to the four restrooms were all in one wall. The two on the left were labeled "Colored Men" and "White Men." I didn't need a chart to know I wasn't white.

Up to that point, the only instruction I had received about the races was a single correction from my mother. She had heard her boys choosing sides and had come out of the house to insist, "It's 'catch a *fellow* by the toe.'" When Paul broke his arm, I was in the first grade at a Catholic school where most of the students were Hispanic. But I didn't know, because I wasn't told, that they were different; except I knew they spoke Spanish as well as English. I wondered how they managed it and thought it was an amazing trick, like using a decoder ring. Speaking Spanish was forbidden in the classroom, but no one could restrain first grade boys during recess. I learned a few useful playground terms. Although I had no idea why they were insulting, tossing them out at appropriate times was as easy as swinging a bat.

I was alone in the restroom. It wasn't dirty, but it wasn't clean either. There were paper towels on the floor near a chock-full trash can. The sinks were without hand soap or hot water and had a grey film around the base of the faucets. Still, it was sterile compared to most gas station restrooms in the 1950s.

A very tall man was waiting for me at the entrance. He had short, curly hair, a rich brown complexion, and dark eyes. He was dressed in clean, neat work clothes. His fists were planted on his hips.

"You don't belong in there. That's not the one for you. You use that one over there. What's wrong with you that you don't know where you belong?"

I was completely baffled.

When I sat next to Marty, he said, "We're not supposed to use the colored one." He was just shy of eighteen months older and therefore knew infinitely more about the world. Years before, he'd taught me how to tie my shoes. "We're White."

"No way."

"It's like that red onion thing. It's just what they call it even if it's purple."

"Well, that's just broken."

SWEET PARTING

In the late spring of 2003, I joined Dad and my remaining siblings in San Antonio, Texas for the funeral of Arthur, my second oldest brother. He had been walking with his grandson at North Star Mall when he suffered a heart attack. He was 54 and had been released from the Navy twenty years earlier due to cardiac issues. He hadn't been willing to admit the problem was real. He had in fact applied almost immediately to the Coast Guard, but he was declined for the same reason.

He refused, as he liked to say, to "take some idiot's opinion to heart." He continued to smoke two packs of Marlboros and drink a sixpack of Budweiser daily. Sausage, bacon, and pizza frequented his plate.

After the memorial service, I told Dad that I would take the opportunity to drive the thirty-five miles to New Braunfels to visit Mom at the Alzheimer's clinic. Unfortunately, my sister Monica overheard and invited herself along. From the moment she arrived at the gathering, she mourned that Arthur hadn't listened to her.

Monica is a universal savior. As an avidly vocal friend of Bill, she has expanded her mission to include insistent advice on every aspect of life from worship through parenting and pasta to driving. For the thirty-five miles, she lectured me about the joys of Jesus, my need to be closer to my son, and the dangers of driving on the expressway.

Loop 410 was under construction. Where the four existing lanes funneled into two, Monica became nervous. She suggested that I shouldn't drive so fast. I was matching the flow of traffic. She insisted it would be better if I got out from between the semis. There was one in front, another behind, and a third to the right. There didn't seem to be an alternative lane unless I drove through the concrete barrier to the left. She condemned me for failing to respect her feelings.

"Monica, the last time I was in an accident was thirty years ago. When was your last?"

She didn't answer. Her husband has a running joke about her body shop repairs being more regular than the utility bills.

At last, we arrived at the nursing home. As soon as we entered, I saw Mom in a wheelchair, part of a group clustered in front of a television. I plopped down in a folding chair beside her and introduced myself.

She smiled indulgently at me and looked away. "I don't believe I know you, sir."

Monica said, "It's too noisy and crowded in here." She grabbed the wheelchair and pushed it out the side door to the patio. I followed.

Monica maneuvered Mom to a round metal table. She took one of the patio chairs. I sat opposite her with Mom on my right.

I asked Mom, "How are you today?"

"Fine as sunshine, sir. And how are you?"

"Doing great."

She smiled. "I don't like you." She giggled like a little girl.

Monica frowned and looked down and away.

I said, "You don't like me?"

"No." She giggled again. "I don't like you."

"Why don't you like me?"

"I don't know. I just don't."

"Are you sure?"

"Yes."

"How do you know? We just met."

"I can feel it."

"There must be a reason. Is it my hair? Or my eyes?"

Lightly she said, "No. Your nose looks funny, but it isn't that."

"There must be a reason"

"I don't know why. I just don't like you." She giggled and covered her mouth.

"What about her?" I pointed at my sister. "Do you like her?"

Monica glared at me. Mom looked at her briefly.

"Oh, her I like, but I don't like you."

"You like her, but not me. Why do you like her?"

"I don't know. I just do."

"Well, I don't blame you. She looks like a nice person."

"Sorta. But—"

Mom stopped and took a long look at Monica. Monica began to squirm. She looked around then suddenly blurted, "Can I get you a drink?" She pointed at a soda machine across the patio.

Mom said, "Do you have coffee? I *love* coffee,"

Monica looked around as if desperate for a cup of coffee.

Mom looked back at me. "You," she said pointing at me with each word, "I don't like you." Then she looked straight ahead, giggled again, and glanced askance at me.

Suddenly her eyes glazed over, and she moved her head up and down in little bounces. She said no more and didn't look at either of us again.

Twenty minutes later, a caretaker came onto the patio. "It's time for Trudy's dinner." She wheeled Mom away.

Monica and I were mostly silent on the way back to San Antonio. Other than pointing out how terrible it was for me to suggest that Mom might not like her she said nothing, not even about the traffic, until I parked in Dad's driveway. "You didn't even tell her you love her."

Mother died a few months later in the middle of the night. I didn't have another opportunity to visit her. If someone had told her the last thing she would say to me was, "I don't like you," she would have giggled.

THE FOX AND THE BOX

Toward sunset, the fox stirred from his slumber and started toward the stream. As he trotted, he planned his night. A hunt for a morsel followed by a survey of his domain sounded like a full and satisfying evening, and if still hungry, he could revisit the rabbit warren near the meadow.

He was startled out of his revery when he arrived at the wide packed-earth path that cut through the forest. A box lay on the far side next to a tree. It was a dull brown, but not nearly as pretty a shade as his own fur. It was longer than his body from snout to tail and wide enough to accommodate his girth.

He had not seen the box the day before, nor was it there in the morning when he had wended his way home from dining at the warren. During the day's full light, the fox had been awakened by a cacophony from the direction of the wide gravel path. He could smell the noxious fumes even from the mouth of his den.

His experience with the creatures who used that path had never been pleasant. Besides their stench, their rudeness was intolerable. Oftentimes when they would see him, they would point and shout and hide their eyes with hands that flashed bright lights. He had learned as a pup that caution was needed around anything abandoned by them. He swore that someday he would find either a new place to live or a way to make those foul creatures disappear.

The fox had completed a wide circumspect quarter circle around the box before he saw, lying with her back legs tucked beside her body and her front paws folded under her chest, a napping ginger cat. The fox stopped, crouched, and watched. He regulated his breath so as to be as quiet as possible, even quieter than he had been when stalking that mouse, so delicious and juicy, last night.

The cat, without turning her head, said, "Too late to slink. I heard you coming five minutes ago." Then she opened her eyes and looked, without searching or hesitation, directly at the fox. "You're as noisy as a dog. You look like one, too."

"I beg your pardon, but there's no reason to get snippy."

"Ah," said the cat, "So you don't like being compared to a dog? Class conscious, eh?"

"I just think they're a bit — misshapen. I think that's the best way to put it without fear of being rude or risking correction. And they really haven't got a coat as fine or fantastic as mine."

"Strange to be so proud of something as dull as brown."

"It is certainly more tasteful than — what is that? Orange?"

"I'm a rich ginger, the most elegant shade imaginable."

The fox decided to leave unceremoniously this uninvited, uncouth intruder. He continued to walk around the box, taking care to maintain a socially significant distance from the cat. But pride got the better of his better judgment. He snarled. "Did your pack throw you out for being catty?"

The cat hissed. "I wasn't ejected. While they went walking, I stepped out of the van to scratch a branch. Then I took a quick snooze on a heap of leaves. When I woke, they were gone."

"Time to reevaluate your place in the pack, eh?"

"I prefer to believe they hadn't noticed I was missing."

"Then why did they leave this box behind for you?"

"That doesn't mean a thing. They drop things like that everywhere."

The fox felt nauseous at the thought of sharing a den with

messy, furless animals. "How can you live with creatures messier than ferrets?"

The cat smoothed her muzzle with a paw. "They're neater at home, but not cleaner. Sometimes the adults lick each other, but they're not very thorough. Did you know they immerse themselves in water almost every day?"

The fox said, "Every day? That seems irrational. Why so often?"

"I have no idea."

"Why expect a cat-keeper to be rational?" The fox tried to mitigate the insult by pretending to laugh. It came off more like a snort.

The cat replied with great pride, "Catering to a cat's whims is not irrational. It's a lifestyle."

The fox regretted his rude remark, unworthy of a species renowned for being clever. Cats were inscrutable. Wanting to regain his own dignity, the fox decided to change the subject. "What's in the box?"

"It's hard to say without looking inside."

"You can't expect me to believe you've never looked inside."

The cat hissed again. "Of course! What do you take me for, an incurious canine? When my cousin from Cheshire visited, he jumped in and closed the lid. When I opened it, there was nothing left of him but his grin. I closed and reopened it. There he was: a cat without a grin."

"Perplexing," said the fox.

"When I asked him where he'd been, he said he'd only come back so I wouldn't be worried about him. Presumptuous of him. We're cats; even our siblings are distant relations. I slammed the lid and haven't opened it since."

"So, he's been trapped in there for how long?"

The cat bared her claws. "It's not locked. He's free to pop out anytime."

"How long?"

"Two weeks."

"Obviously, you haven't stood guard the entire time. Maybe he escaped already."

"He's not a prisoner."

"What I meant is, maybe he doesn't know he can get out while the lid is shut."

As if in profound thought, the cat purred, "HmmMmmMmmm."

The fox scratched behind his left ear. "Did he take food or water with him?"

"No."

"I don't smell death or droppings. How curious—."

The cat stood, arched her back, walked around the box twice. "Let's look inside."

The cat's ear flicked forward, motioning the fox to come close. When the fox stood beside the cat, the cat's paw flipped the lid. They both gingerly peeked inside.

The box was empty.

The cat purred, "HmmMmmMmMm."

The fox snorted. "He must have left while you were nap—"

"I know everything that happens in my domain. Besides, he's not the type to shut a lid behind him."

"Then where is he?"

The cat sat. "Iiifff—" and the cat trailed into silence. Suddenly, she said, "One of us must be inside the closed box to see if there's a concealed panel that's only visible in the dark."

"I take it you mean me," said the fox.

"Although we cats are famous for our ability to see in the dark, I have more experience operating the lid."

"We've already seen that cat existence becomes unstable, as unseemly as that seems. A fox just might be the better choice."

"Exactly."

"What if it's a trap?" The fox spoke out loud but more to himself than to the cat.

The cat grinned like her Cheshire cousin. "I swear on my honor as a felicitous and faithful feline that I will open the lid in fifteen seconds."

"Faithful?"

"Put no credence in those rumors. We cats are loyal in our own way."

The fox thought long and hard. "Let's do it." He jumped in the box, crouched, and said, "Don't make me regret this."

The cat laughed then slammed the lid. She counted the seconds slowly. At seventeen, she flipped open the box top.

The tremulous fox looked into the cat's eyes. "What a relief. I wasn't sure I could trust you."

The cat said, "One more time."

"Why?"

"The question is whether there's a secret compartment. That's yes or no, so we have to ask it at least twice."

"But what if—"

The cat slammed the lid again and counted, "One chimpanzee. Two chimpanzees. . . ."

When the cat opened the box and peeked timorously inside, all she saw was the bottom of the box. "HmmMmmMmMm." She hopped inside, hooked her claws on the lid, and shut it. After fifteen seconds, she pushed the lid open. There was nothing but impenetrable darkness outside. "Oh my," she said. "Curiouser and curiouser." She retreated into the box and let the lid close again.

"—it's you who disappears?" the fox asked, but the lid was already shut before he finished the question.

The fox counted the seconds. At fifteen, the box was still shut. He wondered when the cat would open the box. Twenty-four more seconds passed. The darkness suddenly expanded and filled with an irregular matrix of trillions of dots of light. He couldn't tell if he was floating or falling, but the sensation of movement was pleasantly smooth, even comforting. As he neared a blue, green, brown, and white planet, he knew he would somehow land softly, cat-like, on his paws.

MATTHEW STRAMOSKI

THE STUFF OF POETRY

I was stationed in Japan in the early eighties on the island of Okinawa. The Air Force had sent me there to defend democracy. It was a temporary three-month assignment which was extended seven times. If I had known I was going to stay two years I would have made an effort to learn enough Japanese to be able to say more than "Good morning" or "Bring me some hot coffee, please."

My part in protecting the world from the impending doom of Communism consisted mainly of pushing buttons on a Burroughs 3700 Computer, which required a climate-controlled room and a specialized team to run it. At my previous station, I had honed my skills at cribbage and euchre, essential duties for an NCO, but the opportunities to play were less frequent due to my work hours.

Each time my tour was extended, the Lieutenant changed my shift, alternating between swing and graveyard. The evening shift was usually too busy, and the other regular computer operator, a Japanese national named Mr. Asato, didn't like playing cards even when the workload was low. During graveyard shift, I was usually alone with nothing to do but check the hygrometer each hour. I was forced by solitude and boredom to indulge in my secret passion. Fortunately, Mr. Asato was not one to gossip, and no one was there after midnight to see me pulling from my knapsack a book.

In the Base Exchange, a single rotating display rack stood in the rearmost corner. Though not completely hidden, I could zip past, scan the titles, and scoop up a few books. If I made my raid early, the chances of being seen by a coworker were almost nil. Each month featured a new author, usually a deceased white man. Jane Austin seemed to be the token female, but George Elliot snuck in under the radar. Inexplicably, Gore Vidal and Truman Capote passed the litmus test of respectability.

I had just finished Capote's *Music for Chameleons.* The review in the *Pacific Stars and Stripes* had called it "the worst book of the decade," so of course I had to read it. In fact, I read it from end to start because the panner had especially hated the final selection. I loved it and returned to the Exchange to devour everything from Capote I could find.

On that foray, a thin volume on the rack's bottom level caught my eye, *The Narrow Road to the Interior,* a translation of a work by the seventeenth century poet, Basho. The English version on the left page faced the Japanese original on the right.

Shortly after midnight, I opened to the first page and was confronted by the first enigma. In preparation for his "journey to the far province," the poet "burned moxa on [his] knees."

I dragged my pocket dictionary from my knapsack. Moxa was not listed in it. I wondered if Basho put the mysterious substance moxa on his knees and then set it on fire or if he knelt before burning it on an altar or in his hearth. The first sounded painful, the second more likely but still as incomprehensible as Rimbaud.

I arrived hopeful and early for my next shift. Airman Stevens bolted before I finished taking off my knapsack.

"Mr. Asato, I wonder if you would help me. I've got a question about a Japanese poem."

"Ah." His smile was shaped like an orange segment, a form which usually warns of impending embarrassment. "Poetry is very hard."

"So true. But I don't even understand this one when it's translated into English."

"Of course not. Poetry is too hard for you, GI."

I smiled with flat, stretched lips and, showing him the page, pointed to the English word.

He took the book, and his eyes moved to the opposite page. He smiled as if pleasantly relieved. "A plant. Used in medicine."

"Was Basho a doctor?"

"Oh, GI." He pointed at his temples with both index fingers. "Turn on lights, get on the stick. Anyone can do. Make a paste, put it on a needle. Stick it in your knee. Set it on fire. It gives strength, clarity, stamina."

I was still puzzled. "It's like an herb?"

"Come. I show you."

We stepped outside. The light above the door illuminated a semispherical area. He pointed at a patch of plants, rampant weeds crouched in a ditch beside the road. "That is moxa."

I couldn't believe it. Mug wort, a common weed in Texas. We used to pull it out of the lawn and toss it into the garbage. I said, "All my life I have been walking on the stuff of poetry, and I did not know it."

He said, nodding wisely, "Crazy GI."

MATTHEW STRAMOSKI

MOLE IN A HOLE

Mr. Mole did not like the sun. The brilliance of its light hurt his tiny eyes and made him squint. When other animals saw him squint, they thought he had bad eyes and a poor intellect. His eyes were poor and his brain was slow, but he did not like it when others noticed. He was afraid they would someday be rude and say mean things to his face. He knew all too well how cruel other animals could be because he had often heard the ridicule heaped on those who looked or acted a little oddly. The jays were especially uncouth.

Although no one had yet said nasty things to his face, he thought they snickered behind his back and winked to each other and pointed at him and imitated his squint. He could not see his back, much less behind it, but he imagined the slights vividly enough to convince himself. It hurt because the others were mean and cowardly. They could not even find the courage to mock him to his face. At least then he would have the chance to defend himself by calling them names and making fun of them in turn.

Mr. Mole loved to dig in the dirt. Not the wet slimy dirt that a pig loves, that stinks of swine sweat and sticks to the skin. Not the coarse dry clay that a fox prefers, that irritates the eyes and makes one sneeze. Mr. Mole adored the feel of damp, cozy loam, rich with leaf and twig. When aged to perfection, in the darkness of the soil, the humus achieved an earthy aroma that brought him contentment and a sense of security. He would sit serenely in the dark, awaiting the faint, delightful plop that meant dinner had fallen from the ceiling.

When he had been old enough to find his own home, he had spent three nights seeking a perfect spot not too far from and not too close to water. He searched in the pine forest, in the fir grove, in the glade, and along the riverbank. Finally, he found what he thought was an ideal location not far from the beaver pond on the stream that flowed from the hills at the edge of the forest to the river that came from and went to places he could not imagine, lands no neighbor had ever visited.

Fantastic tales of bizarre creatures and plants, of waterless rivers and salty ponds, of cold worse than winter and heat more intense than summer were told and retold, passed from the edges of the forest to his threshold. He turned away those who bore the uncomfortable news that mystery, excitement, even danger thrived somewhere in the world. But the squirrels chattered the tales, and the chipmunks squeakily repeated them. The jays shrieked their own distorted, vulgar versions, and woodpeckers tapped out the horrors. Each had their own way to spread rumors, and all of the ways were impossible for Mr. Mole to ignore. He tried to turn away, to burrow until he was unable to hear them anymore, but his curiosity eventually brought him to listen, clandestinely if he could manage it.

Once, when he was discovered, he shrugged and turned up his nose as best he could manage with his sloping shoulders and his slim nose. He snuffled and pretended to be disgusted.

"You talk too much about things you don't know. Have you nothing better to do?"

The very idea that there might be something better to do had not occurred to most of them.

A squirrel sat up on her hind legs and curled her tail questioningly. "I have enough nuts in storage. The kits have scampered off to be on their own. It's not mating season. What did you have in mind?"

Two chipmunks ran up to Mr. Mole but lost interest when

they realized he wasn't going to feed them.

A jay leaned rigidly forward and squawked. "Are you scolding us? Who made you king of the hill?"

A tortoise said, "Slow down there, buddy. You don't know what I don't know. There's more to me than meets the eye."

A hare racing by stopped short. "You're jumping to conclusions, my friend. I've been to the edge and back, and I can tell you: There isn't here, and that's not this."

An owl hiding in a fir hooted and said, "Who's this smarty pants?"

A fox, ears pricked, crouched low and tried to sneak up on Mr. Mole, but he caught the fox's scent and retreated into his burrow. The fox dug swiftly at the hole but couldn't catch up. He left muttering under his breath, "His meat is probably too tough anyway."

Mr. Mole visited his larder where he squeezed and ate the last six earthworms he had stored.

"Food is getting scarce here. Best to move along."

He dug a tunnel this way and that until he felt he was far away. He avoided the surface because he liked being underground and preferred to be alone.

None of the other animals missed him.

MATTHEW STRAMOSKI

THE APRIL FOOL'S DAY HIKE

I was furious. Some work-related matter that seemed threatening had set me off. That it was beyond my control only made me angrier.

The excess energy felt like sandpaper rubbing me. I drove at a mostly reasonable speed to the Mission Creek Preserve. Luckily there were no markings on the gravel parking lot, so I could with a good conscience take what normally would have been two spaces. I slung my daypack over my shoulder and shrugged it on as I stomped down the trail.

I had a lot to say to certain jerks, and I said it with an amount of sophisticated subtlety I was sure they couldn't possibly comprehend even if I had said it aloud. I tossed in a few gratuitous vulgarities that were closer to their level. They answered stupidly; I retorted cleverly; they made wildly illogical leaps; I refuted them with sound sarcasm.

So deeply was I involved in arguing with people who weren't there that I wasn't present either. Striding down the trail, eyes blurred to the surroundings, focused on the absent, gesturing emphatically, not looking where I was going as I passed a bush beside the trail.

Then I heard the rattle.

I looked down.

A rattlesnake was unwinding barely two inches from my right foot. I'm exaggerating. It was three inches away. It was uncoiling from a figure eight, the diamond pattern on its back blurred yet discernible, its upright tail clattering.

I screamed like a toddler and jumped away. I swear I covered twelve feet in three steps, looking down and behind, both eyes riveted on the rattler. I came to a stop, my breath shallow and short, heart pounding, hands shaking.

The snake's body was stretched in a line pointing its tail towards me and curving the head back like the crook of a shepherd's staff. The triangular head was lowered as if aiming at me, keeping me in its sights, ready.

An older brother had once told me a snake could only strike twice its length, which isn't true at all, but I had at least one length to spare. I was far enough away to be beyond an immediate strike. I knew I probably wasn't entirely safe, but I also recognized that it was more frightened of me than I of it.

It stayed stationary for perhaps a minute, rattling, hissing at me. I had never heard a snake hiss before and felt surprised that it was more than a legend. It was more intimidating than the hiss of a cat, amped by its more ominous overtones.

Now knowing I was at a safe distance, I was struck by how beautiful its flattened round body was, the regularity of its brown and tan pattern, the sleekness of its scales, the symmetry of its triangular head.

Without moving its eyes from me, it began to slide away into the bush, a movement that seemed without method, as if transported across the ground on a hiss, an exhalation, a whisper. When hidden completely in the bush, it became silent.

I let a few minutes pass, savoring the experience. Awe had calmed my heart, stilled my hands, and slowed my breath.

Once I felt safe, I circled the bush at a respectful distance, searching, wondering how it was hidden, but I couldn't see the snake.

I realized that I had gone off on a seldom traveled trail without telling anyone where I was headed, without a cellphone, without much sense at all.

That matter at work now seemed trivial.

THE PRIEST'S DOG'S TALE

People call me Caleb. I suspect they either can't hear well or can't enunciate clearly. My friends call me H-h-h-h. My twenty-eighth ex, at the end of our ten-second affair, referred to me as Krrr. Last week, my twenty-ninth ex called me the same when she realized I would not help raise the pups. (None of the fathers involved in that litter volunteered either.) Of course, being a fine, exemplary member of the pack, I readily answer to all three names as well as the one my mother called me, which cannot be said without slobbering affectionately.

I am the fifth in my line to be called Caleb. My father, Caleb the Sleek, has passed on the family history during this interminable trek across the desert wilderness east of Egypt. Mine is a proud heritage in spite of a blotch or two.

We are descended from Caleb the Fanged, Breaker of Boundaries. He stood thigh-high to a giraffe when his ears were pricked up. His golden-brown coat, fiercely erect tail, and bone-white teeth impressed even the hyenas. At only two years old, he mercilessly slaughtered seven sacred kittens in the courtyard of the Temple of Anubis, a proud moment in canine history. He subsequently mated, without divine approval, with the Temple's Principal Jackal. He escaped the outraged priests, barged upriver, and disappeared into the wilds of Nubia. Unsubstantiated legends about the feats of Caleb, Prince of Hyenas, have flowed downriver in a steady stream ever since.

The Temple Jackal bore him two sons. The elder son, Canubis the Most High, was offered as a burnt sacrifice to appease the offended deity. Anubis found the aroma pleasing; his wrath calmed; the need for further appeasement died. The offering might have been less pleasing had the priests first killed the dog. The younger son, Caleb the Cranky, my great-grandfather, witnessed the sacred rite of atonement. It affected his temperament adversely.

When he was barely three months old, he was given as a pet to the Chief Priest's daughter. He made the mistake of biting her hand as she tried to feed him dried meat mixed with sour milk and ground honeybees. In retaliation, she sold him into slavery to a Jewish family a week before they were forced to relocate.

Thus began our family's nomadic life. Caleb the Cranky lived to an old age, twenty-five in human years, and fathered more pups, as he is reputed to have claimed, than he could count. Our family lore reveals that he never managed to reckon past three, so I suspect the Cranky was no more prolific than most other dogs. Still his bragging was never questioned to his snout. He was already sufficiently ill-tempered.

His eldest son, Caleb the Fat, spent most days riding on the back of the cart with the dirty bedding and most nights lying guard at the entrance to the family tent. He was notoriously ineffective as a sentinel. The kindest reports state that he barked on two occasions when thieves tried to steal his food bowl and growled once when a child pulled his tail. After his third birthday, he had grown so ungainly he had to be hoisted onto the cart by two stout men. His heart gave out when he reached ten human years. As he lay dying, Caleb the Cranky stole his bone. His only recognized son was my father, Caleb the Sleek, renowned for the luster of his coat and the profundity of his scintillating black eyes. He excelled at diplomacy: he knew just how to wag his tail to appear inviting and cuddly.

We had been following a visionary for longer than any of

the canines had been alive, thirty-five years if the donkeys could be believed. The terrain was beginning to look familiar even to those with a short lifespan. The cows (who had learned early not to stick their necks out) quietly complained to Dad about the lack of green fodder, the scarcity of water, and the apparent randomness of direction. At that point, it had not occurred to any of the canine contingent that we could do anything more than follow the leader of the pack. But the cattle's persistent pleas moved my father.

When a dog begins to question the leader, it's usually for mating rights, but (as my father so kindly put it) the leader's wife was not bad looking as far as humans go, but she was no dog. Clearly, Dad's motives were altruistic, focused on what would benefit the entire pack. Not prone to rashness, he quietly observed how the humans went about making decisions.

Most days we didn't break camp. The unofficial word was that we were following a cloud, a sign which is rare in the desert. When we did move, the Aleph Male seemed riveted by a puff of white, usually near the horizon. It always outpaced us and sometimes simply vanished into the blue sky, contorting and dwindling in what appeared to be a display of petulance. Then everyone halted and awaited a new sign. Frequently, we heard the humans mumbling about "moving in mysterious ways." They can be obtuse.

Like an expert diplomat, Dad waited until he understood how to manipulate his target. He began to follow the leader wherever he went. Each morning the Aleph and his older brother would observe from the top of the closest hill the horizon in all directions and then either order a march or return to their tents. The elder seemed unusually deferential to his kid brother who insisted on getting his way every time. The younger would begin his search of the sky in what appeared to be a random direction. It was no wonder that the trek was haphazard.

My father, a brilliant strategist and master manipulator, realized that he needed to take surreptitious control. While the Aleph broke his fast, Dad would sit beside him, tongue lolling, bright eyes gazing upward in feigned admiration, tail wagging in a blatant appeal for affection. If unnoticed, he would beat his tail against the tent floor, even go so far as to plop his muzzle on Aleph's unwashed thigh, or, as a last resort, whimper as if his heart's contentment depended on a simple pat on the head, his life's purpose fulfilled by a casual caress. Humans are easily seduced by overt devotion, no matter what the ulterior motive.

Soon, he was a welcome companion on the daily expedition to search for a cloud to follow. Aleph would call, "Come on, boy," and the elder brother, ever happy with being second, would encourage, "Lead the way, boy."

Dad quickly discovered that they were more easily led if he pretended to investigate a swath instead of moving directly toward the hilltop. Occasionally, the elder would find a stick on the ground and amuse himself with a toss and a cry: "Fetch." His aim was terrible, but Dad always pretended the throw was perfectly executed. If he tossed it too far afield, Dad would pretend to chase it but instead would curve in the direction of the true destination. There he would stand straight and tall, head perked and tail wagging, looking eager for the brothers to join him, barking when their limited attention span would drift. The elder never seemed to notice the interruption in the game, apparently losing interest in the stick rather easily.

When the group assembled at the hilltop, the final, crucial maneuver would be flawlessly executed. Rather than allow them to be distracted by a random puff in the sky, he would growl, bark, crouch, dash forward a few steps, as if riveted by something on the horizon in the same direction they had last traveled. The elder was usually the more curious. "What is it, boy? A rabbit?" Then to his younger brother, "He's caught the scent of something. A rabbit, I bet."

Dad would continue to display animated signs hoping his feigned excitement would draw the attention of the Aleph, not letting up until the Aleph would point and shout, "There! That's the way!"

He often got it right.

Still, five years elapsed "wandering."

Finally, the Aleph stood on a hilltop and gazed across a valley with a narrow, shallow "river," hardly big enough for a dozen dogs to bath in. The old man sighed heavily then proclaimed, "Darn it, we're in sight of the promised land."

A much younger man, who had become second after Aleph's elder brother mysteriously died naked on a hilltop, asked, "What's the problem? Isn't this what we set out to find?"

The Aleph slowly shook his head and shooed away a fly. "I thought—well, I—." He sighed again.

The younger man said, "What? You were expecting chopped dates? We take what we're given." He turned away from the valley and faced the Aleph. "What's really bothering you?"

"I was told I would die when I came to see the promised land," said the Aleph, "because I stutter-tapped a rock. It wasn't really my fault. I've got an allergy and happened to sneeze at just the wrong moment."

"Didn't you explain?"

"There are some in this universe who don't care about excuses. They're the same ones who get picky about the small stuff. So be careful and listen closely to instructions. If you're feeling under the weather, you might want to put things off for a day or two."

The two humans gazed contemplatively to the west. The young man broke the silence. "I thought it would be—I don't know, more inviting? greener?"

The Aleph pointed with the butt of his staff. "Are those people? Is that a city?"

"Don't worry," the younger man said. "I'll take care of it. I think we could get the place for a song."

Caleb the Sleek nuzzled the younger man's right hand, and I followed along, licking the left. It's always a good idea to lead the one who'll be in charge tomorrow.

REQUIEM

"**W**here's Jim Morrison?" The young man's question annoyed and puzzled me. He wore tennis shoes, blue jeans, and a sweatshirt.

I was standing alone and silent in front of Chopin's grave admiring the sorrowful muse, as elegantly sculpted as his music. I had come from the tomb of Bizet and was about to search for Bellini's.

The cemetery, Père Lachaise, is in Paris, but the man had made no attempt to speak French or even to ask if I spoke English. Just finishing my third week in France and trying to use my meager French whenever I could, my brain was at the point where it was ready to go snowy like a television set at three in the morning before cable, so I should have been glad for the easy moment. Instead, I felt a resentment that he was fertilizing the rumors of American arrogance and insensitivity.

I was also puzzled. I had heard the name before, somewhere, but I couldn't tell you who he was or why I had heard of him. I only listened to the radio while driving, and there were only two stations preset: NPR and the classical music station.

Not wishing to lecture him about courtesy and having little incentive to find out who this Morrison was, I asked, "You're looking for a grave?"

The young man's face passed from puzzled to amused. "Yeah."

I dug the official guide out of my inside jacket pocket. To my surprise, Morrison was listed in the index. I cross-referenced the map. "We're here and he's there." I pointed out two points on the map. "I don't know for sure," I said, "but it looks like it might be that way."

Alone again, I went in search of Bellini's tomb. Before I found it, another young man, dressed similarly to the first, called to me from a distance. "Hey! Where's Jim Morrison?"

As I was approaching Rossini's mausoleum, a third young man waved me down. "Excuse me. Where's Jim Morrison?"

I wondered what gave these seekers the impression that I was an English speaker. When the fourth young man in tennis shoes, blue jeans, and a sweatshirt asked me the same question, I was just turning away from the exquisite canopy over the combined tombs of Heloise and Abelard: four gables supported on columns, rose windows without stained glass, and a central spire topped with a cross: Josephine Bonaparte's tribute to separated lovers.

I decided to delay my visit to Oscar Wilde's Egyptian angel until I had seen this resting place of Jim Morrison. Certainly, when I returned to the States and revealed that I had been to Pere Lachaise, I would be asked to tell all about my insincere pilgrimage.

On the way, I passed an elderly man. He was weeping and his face was contorted. He had genuflected to place a bouquet on a gravestone and was struggling to get on his feet. A somewhat younger woman, perhaps his daughter, helped him to his feet. In his left hand, he clutched a black beret. His black pants, several inches too long, bunched twice between his knees and ankles. As he turned, I saw his dark eyes, wide as if in disbelief, unfocused, unseeing. I heard feeble yet heartfelt sobs. I tried to be unobtrusive as I passed. I read the stone at the head of the simple marble block: Simone Signoret, Yves Montand. These visitors did not ask me where Morrison was.

I found the grave I had been asked about. It was a simple block of stone with a Greek inscription under his name and dates. There were flowers, rocks, papers with and without plastic covers, photos of James Douglas Morrison, and many items whose significance was known only to the donors. I wondered what the Greek inscription meant and resolved to investigate once I was home again. Like a New Year's resolution, the promise remained unfulfilled.

When I returned home, not one person asked me if I had seen the Holy Grail of Americans' Graves.

A lmost 15 years later, I gave a deep tissue massage to a new client. My CD with massage music had finally died, so I borrowed another from the pile at the spa manager's office.

After leading the client to the massage room and finding out what he wanted from his treatment, I told him, "I had to borrow this CD. I don't know what's on it. If it's a problem, I can turn it off or go find another one."

He was sure it wouldn't matter.

As I worked on him, he told several funny stories. Perhaps he needed to distract himself from the discomfort of a undeniably deep massage. What music was playing finally registered on me at the fourth track. I asked, "Is that *Dies Irae*?"

"Yeah, every track so far," he said. "I'll know you're a sadist if you start dancing to it."

We laughed. He told more humorous anecdotes.

There was a trend in his stories, so I asked, "Pardon me for asking, but I can't help noticing that you talk about drugs a lot. Do you or did you have a problem with drugs?" It was a bold, risky question to ask a client, but he seemed like someone who wouldn't mind. And I do sometimes ask really inappropriate personal questions, but if he was still a user, it would influence how forceful the massage would be.

He said, "No. I never did. I used to be part of a band, and every day, when I went to work, I saw an example of what drugs will do to you."

"A band? Would I know it?"

"Maybe. It was The Doors."

I repeated the name a couple times, searching my memory, knowing there was some connection. "Oh! Wasn't that with Jim Morrison?"

"That's the one. I watched while he destroyed himself."

"You know, when I was at Pere Lachaise, people kept asking me, 'Where's Jim Morrison?'"

The client, flat on his back, said loudly and with finality, "He's nowhere. He's dead."

THE BELLES' APPEAL

Mary Jo and Mary Lou were simply devastated when they learned that the god-like General Robert Edward Lee had proven to be nothing better than a god-awful quitter. They found it incomprehensible that such an impeccably well-mannered, well-dressed gentleman would give up the Noble Cause while yet one of his soldiers had a life to sacrifice and strength enough to gasp his last.

With suppressed chagrin, Mary Jo donned last year's Easter bonnet, which she had been forced to modify rather than replace the previous year. It was only by the demands of decency that her twice-dyed skirt concealed the frayed tassels on her shoes. The unavailability of supplies caused by the godless Yankee's disruption of civilization was making life unbearably unfashionable.

Mary Lou fastened her bonnet under her chin and feigned surprise that it was missing the ribbon on the left that had been shaped like a petunia. Brave in the face of adversity, she swirled her parasol over her head, crossed the veranda, and descended the seventeen steps to the dust that had been her rose garden. "I do declare it looks like sunshine will drench us today."

Mary Jo shut the double wide doors behind them. She sighed, remembering how, not so long ago, she had never had to think about closing a door. Now, at the end of all she held dear, she had to sweep her voluminous skirts aside with one hand while pulling the door shut with the other. "Chin up, sister belle. And hold your parasol proudly."

The sisters stepped as lightly as wounded does onto the uneven ground that had once been the smooth carriage way. Their skirts rustled as they hightailed it to the dilapidated barn where they yoked the decrepit donkey to the buggy as best they could. They drove the beast along the most direct lane, between the charred, unplowed, and unplanted fields, to the neighboring plantation.

They paused on the stoop to catch their breath and shake off the red dust and withered blades. When Lily swung open the door, wide enough to accommodate their skirts, the sisters concealed their astonishment. The common knowledge was that all the slaves had fled, frightened by the prospect of freedom forced on them by barbarian Yankees.

Mary Beth received them in her parlor. Under her billowy skirt, which she was embarrassed to admit even to herself had been seen before by the sisters, she was secretly clad in her finest, naughtiest article of clothing, her last surviving black pantaloons. "Before you say anything about that wicked business in the Sovereign State of Virginia, I must apologize for the way I am dressed." She felt it imperative to explain what some might misconstrue as the limited state of her wardrobe. "It's laundry day, and all my elegance is being boiled."

After the sisters suppressed an outright display of knowing glances and smiles between themselves, they sobbed, in unison, "I do declare—" then both paused politely.

Mary Jo invited with a wisp of a gesture, "You first, sister belle."

"I do declare, indeed I do, I think I cannot comprehend in the least how General Lee could possibly surrender——yes, I am forced to dare say that horrid, unthinkable word out loud ——*surrender* while a single noble Son of the South yet lives and breathes."

"Inconceivable sacrilege!" Mary Jo took up the thread while Mary Lou took in a breath and clasped the ivory brooch at her heaving bosom of which she was very proud. It bore the likeness of a certain ancestor who, if spurious rumors could be believed, may have earned two places in her family tree.

Mary Lou had regained her breath. "Be*tray*al is what it is! Whether sworn or not, they knew we weak ones expected, and therefore it was their implicit promise, expected them to win or die. How could they choose ignominity?"

Mary Beth suggested gently, "Ignominy?"

Mary Jo asserted, "Yes! Ignobility and ignoramusness incarnate!"

In a whisper Mary Lou dared speak the unspeakable. "It is said (forgive my sinful ears for having heard it for I strive each day to hear no evil but even the sweetest of girls cannot help what is said around them) ——. Why just the other day, little Billy Joe used a vulgar term to refer to a peashooter. I couldn't help but imagine ——." She hushed, cleared her throat, and asked delicately, "Where was I?"

"It is said ——," prompted Mary Beth with a kind and patient gaze, her head leaning forward and her right hand suggesting an airy semicircle.

"You've heard it too, then? Oh. I see." Mary Lou drew a fan from her sleeve to conceal her blush. "As I was saying, it is said the Slaves shall be unshackled, turned free, unbound——"

Mary Jo could not restrain her compassion. "The poor, hopeless dears!"

Mary Lou placed the back of her hand against her forehead, a gesture she felt perfectly expressed her ineffable fear for the Universe. "Let loose in the world to——"

Mary Beth interrupted. "With no one to guide and coddle them! What will they do? Where will they go?" She dabbed delicately with a monogrammed handkerchief at the corner of her eye, unable to control her desperate fear for the future of her dear ones. So overtaken with emotion was she that she allowed the sisters to hear her two quick, sorrowful sobs. They flushed and quickly adjusted the curls cascading from under their bonnets.

Mary Jo said confidentially, "Why, Mary Beth Addison, is that a C on your handkerchief?"

Mary Beth pretended the impertinence had not been spoken. "What shall we do, my dears, to help set the world right again?"

Mary Lou, wringing her hands, said with only the tiniest quiver in her voice, "We must cease the day, rise up, and defend the rights of our slaves to remain in their place."

Mary Jo concurred vigorously, "We must not let anyone force freedom on them."

"But they are so easily fooled! Can you imagine their believing they can make their own choices?" Mary Lou restrained her need to knit her brows in consternation, for fear the wrinkles would set in permanently before she could marry.

"And they are useless at fighting. They don't even know which end of a knife to hold, much less a gun."

Mary Lou agreed. "It's due to lack of experience, some say."

"Why think so?" asked Mary Beth.

"Back in Africa, they are reputed to be adept with spears, so it only follows——"

Mary Jo interrupted. "No, no! They are so inept with weapons they are a danger to themselves and everyone around them. There is no telling what might occur. Why just the other Tuesday, Mr. O'Connor of Thirteen Loblollies made the grave mistake of asking his boy to hold his rifle for him while he indulged his Mammie's unspoken desire."

Such foolishness in a grown man astonished Mary Beth. "Surely he didn't do! I would have thought he'd leave it laying on the ground."

"The boy claimed it was handed to him by the man himself, and there was no one to contradict him save common sense itself. Mammie said she couldn't see anything but straw."

Mary Beth sighed. "I reckon we will never know."

"Then the silly ninny accidentally shot the old dear right between the eyes——from behind."

Mary Lou sadly confirmed her sister's account. "The upshot was the boy claimed he stumbled while polishing the trigger."

"My-oh-my," said Mary Beth. "I heard tell of the tragedy Wednesday last. Where did they bury him?"

Mary Jo looked surprised. "Bury? They fed him to the hogs, of course."

Mary Beth brushed the air with her open hand. "Why, silly-be-thee! I meant Mr. O'Connor."

"Most of him is stored in the loft. The carpenter plans to use the splattered wall boards in his coffin to keep his body whole for the Last Judgment."

Mary Beth said gravely, "When is the funeral? I would dearly love to attend, although I haven't a thing to wear." She had nothing in black except her pantaloons.

"Reverend Blackwood is still searching his agenda for a free moment."

Mary Lou said, "Mr. O'Connor should have practiced his Sunday skills more religiously."

"At least he was on his knees when he came to glory." Mary Jo turned her eyes heavenward.

"Amen to that, sister belle."

Mary Beth tinkled a delicate rococo bell. "Let us toast his memory. Anyone care for a shot of bourbon?"

The three women took the opportunity to toast as well the departed Sons of the South who had passed in glory beyond the reach of the shame of disgraceful surrender. They lauded the women of Vicksburg who had endured starvation rather than give in until the very moment the men surrendered. They saluted the bravery of those who had retreated with grace and dignity, believing they would fight another day, only to be betrayed by that quitter Lee. The whiskey bottle was now empty, so they toasted no one else.

"But we," said Mary Beth, "must find a way to save the Noble Cause."

"Obviously it was beyond the abilities of mere men, but what weapons have we to offer besides feminine wiles?" asked

Mary Jo.

Mary Lou said indignantly, "Those I will not bestow on Yankee swine!" She hiccupped and smiled at the fireplace logs.

"I have heard tell," Mary Jo whispered, "of an army of slaves, to the north of the North, who could be used to continue the fight."

"Slaves to fight the Abolitionists?" asked Mary Beth.

"These are happy slaves who are good with their hands."

Mary Beth was puzzled. "But, Mary Jo, aren't all slaves ——?"

Mary Lou interrupted. "Where are they? How do we buy them?"

"They're at the North Pole, but they're not for sale. We'll have to steal them."

Mary Lou shrugged. "They may as well be at the bottom of the sea. No one but Santa Clause can get to the Pole."

Mary Jo said, "Silly-be-thee, not even he! They're at the magnetic north pole. All we need are huskies and sleds, and they are common enough."

Mary Lou wanted to protest being seen in anything as common as dogsleds (although they were hardly common in those temperate parts), but before she could speak, Mary Jo clapped her hands and said triumphantly, "Attack the North from the north! They will never see us coming."

Gazing into the depths of her empty glass, Mary Lou exclaimed, "Why you are as bright as you are pretty! Don't you agree, Mary Beth?"

Mary Beth leaned forward, her brows knit and her lips parted as if she were considering being contrary.

Mary Jo held up a hand. "Now, let's just slow our mule team to a trot before that wagon overturns. I saw in a book that I almost read in its entirety that there is no North Pole at all. Up where those Elves are supposed to be holed up, there's a gigantic hole. It opens to where Eden was from the moment of creation, although the Earth's center is hollow now, like a cookie jar that's been raided."

"Why, that can't be," said Mary Lou.

Mary Jo nodded vigorously. "It's been proven by scientific speculation. The book was by Dr. Quickly himself, and it came with a free bottle of his Milk of Magnetic Love."

Mary Lou wagged her finger. "Don't y'all know he's a Yankee?"

Mary Jo gasped and clasped her pendant. "The lying sludge!"

Mary Beth cleared her pale white, feminine throat with ladylike grace. "Ladies, Santa Clause doesn't really exist, and neither do his elves. That's nothing more than a way to pass the blame when your parents buy a stupid gift."

Mary Jo fired a perplexed look at the cold hearth. "Then who set the tree ablaze last year?"

Mary Lou patted her sister's knee. "Never you trouble yourself about it, sister belle. Mama told me in confidence. Grandfather accidentally ignited it when he was lit."

Mary Beth said, "I heard tell it was your father."

"Exactly right," said Mary Lou. She lifted her empty glass to her rose-red lips, then returned it to her lap untasted. "Since we cannot count on anyone but ourselves, we must prepare to defend our virtues."

Mary Jo shook her head as if freeing herself from a conundrum. "We will need rifles and ammunition. But I haven't any ready money except five million greybacks, and that won't even buy water from a creek."

Mary Beth said, "Ladies, we can sell our jewelry to finance the rearmament."

Mary Lou said, "I'm afraid our plans may be getting too big for our brooches." The back of her left hand pressed her forehead and her right clasped her locket. "There is so very little that remains of my finery. How to part from the last, sacred memento of my dearly departed father?"

Mary Jo whispered, "Grandfather."

"Yes, sister belle, Father was grand to us both."

Mary Jo looked confused.

Mary Beth sedately cleared her throat. "We shall raid Thirteen Loblollies on our way. The dead have a way of being useful if you're quick enough."

Mary Lou shook her head. "Mrs. O'Connor hightailed it to Jackson yesterday."

Mary Beth inhaled slowly and gave a lengthy sigh. "Mary Jo, there's another bottle in that knitting basket."

BIRDIE BYE

My mother's gentle touch on my shoulder woke me on the first day of first grade. She said cheerfully, "Time for school! How exciting!" Then she followed my gaze to the birdcage on my desk. My parakeet had become a pile of assorted feathers at the bottom of its cage. Her smile became frozen. "Well," she said, "grab your clothes and change in the bathroom." When I brought my pajamas back to the room, the cage was gone.

Breakfast was quieter than usual for our family. No one said anything about the missing bird until my older brother Jim left the table. He sniggered, "I guess we don't need to feed the cat today."

Mother said, "Get moving. We don't want to be late the first day."

When we arrived at school, Jim sprinted across the lawn toward his friends. Mother took me by the hand and walked with me to my classroom. A nun stood at the door. "And what would your name be?"

I stared open-mouthed up at the monolith.

My mother answered for me.

The nun smiled down on me. "Just take a seat anywhere."

I went silently to the nearest unoccupied desk.

Starting time arrived. "My name is Sister Mary Jonathum. That's Jona*thum* just like your *thumb*." She held her thumb high above her head.

An hour passed as we were each assigned our proper seat, told where to put our personal items, and led through the rigors of learning the rules and covering our textbooks with heavy brown paper. I stored my school supplies in my desk, as instructed, and then marched with the other kids behind the teacher to the playground.

I hung back on the sidewalk, watched my classmates, and listened to the bustle and clamor from the merry-go-round and swings. I could hear pigeons cooing nearby.

Sister Mary Jonathum approached, a broad smile dimpling her cheeks. "Don't you want to play?"

I didn't know what to say, so I said, "No."

Her smile changed into a concerned line, and she knitted her brows. "Is something wrong?"

I looked away from her. A sparrow bathed in the dust beyond the water fountain. "Nothing. I'm tired."

"Well. Come and join us when you're ready. Get to know the other kids. It'll be fun, exciting."

"Okay."

I did not move until my mother arrived.

As we walked to the car, she asked, "Did you tell anyone about the parakeet?"

"No."

My mother nodded. "I understand. It's best to keep your problems buried. No one wants to carry someone else's burden."

THE OLD MAN AND THE BIG WOOD RIVER

He was an old man and he had driven for 84 miles without taking a pee break. His wife had tried to keep up a congenial conversation for the first 40 miles but then had surrendered to reality. Her neighbor who lived two trailers to the south had said the old man was gruñón, which is the worst kind of grouchy, having no discernable cause and therefore no known cure.

The old man was short and gaunt with facial wrinkles and the suggestion of a wattle. Next to his ears and across his cheeks were random blotches of brown and tan. His bald crown had an almost unblemished complexion having been protected from the sun his entire adult life by a combover and a Yankees baseball cap. His arms, which had once been muscular and tanned from outdoor work, and his legs, which had always remained covered even in sultry times, looked like little more than bones wrapped loosely in corduroy.

The wife had brought a Triple-A folding map which she had carried to the car in a bag slung over her shoulder. The bag was a soft tan, fabricated with a sturdy corded fabric after a pattern she had found on the internet. He had insisted that he didn't need the map. He had already consulted one online and it was indelibly in his memory. She snuck it out of the bag and hid it in the glove compartment while he packed the camping gear in the trunk.

They drove north on the main highway out of Twin Falls. At Ketchum, as they passed the cemetery on their right, the old man looked to the left and reminded the wife how dissatisfied they had been with the service at the hotel where they had stayed two years ago. Although he was looking at the hotel, he could not remember its name.

The wife reminded him that this was their first visit to Ketchum; the hotel had been in Moab, three years ago before the pandemic began.

"Yes," he said without smiling. "I remember it now. There was a donut shop across the street, not a cemetery."

"Easy to confuse," she said.

North of Ketchum, the highway angled north-northwest, roughly paralleling the Big Wood River. Between the river and the highway, hedges and walls blocked the view, but through the gaps and gates, the old man caught glimpses of impeccable lawns and impressive mansions constructed mostly of stone, resembling the estates of English nobility. The old man envied the rewards of wealth; suspected most owners had worked hard to inherit from obnoxious, greedy, powerful relatives; and wished his brow sweat could have been exchanged for gold, at a pound for an ounce. Like his past and his prospects, the sweat had evaporated and left behind only a distasteful residue.

Soon after the hedges gave way to brush and forest, the wife motioned ahead and to the right. "That's our turn."

"Of course," he said. The residual nastiness of his thoughts colored his tone, but the wife remained unfazed.

The road was paved for first few hundred yards. It passed the parking lot for the Visitor Center, the side road leading to the residences for park personnel, and then the windsock for a heliport that more closely resembled an open field. The road became well maintained graded dirt. A mile and a half farther they found on the right the entrance to Murdoch Campground.

She said, "Let's try this one."

He grunted, turned in and passed the information stand on the left without pausing. At the first campsite, she said it looked nice, but he objected, "No place for the tent."

"How about the grassy spot yonder?"

"A marsh if it rains."

She liked a site on the edge of the forest, but he thought it was too far from the sole vault toilet. All the others were taken. On the second drive through, they chose to camp on the edge.

Before the old man backed into the parking slot, the wife got out and stood at the picnic table, out of the way. The slot obliqued halfway along its length where it was flanked by a pine on one side and a small boulder on the other. He backed up, looking from the rearview to the side mirrors. His neck and back were too stiff to turn enough in the seat to look over his shoulder. He zigzagged, too close to the tree, too close to the rock, until his seat was even with the trunk. He got out, walked to the rear of the car, looked first at the table and then at the tent site, judged them both to be too distant, got in the car and backed it up three yards. He then began to unpack the gear from the trunk onto the table.

"Where do you want the tent?" the wife asked.

"Right there." He pointed to a spot between a cluster of pines and the firepit.

"It's not even ground."

"It'll be fine with the air mattresses."

She took a short broom from the backseat of car and swept away as many twigs and pebbles as she could. The old man took the opportunity to walk to the vault toilet. When he returned, his wife said, "There's a root sticking out here. Looks gnarly if you ask me."

He smiled indulgently. "It'll be fine. Why don't you go and register us?"

"Doesn't the Campground Host come round in the evening?"

"If you need the Senior Pass card, I've got it."

He struggled the tent out of the trunk, hauled it to the chosen spot, and dropped it. Bending with a suppressed groan, he spread the tent flat, staked the corners, and popped it open before securing the guy ropes with bent stakes and an adjacent tree branch. He rested a moment sitting on the picnic table's bench. Its rigid wood felt hard and he could feel the ridges against his hip bones.

He had personally chosen the forest green tent because it was spacious for two people: nine feet square and at the center half a head taller than the old man on a good day. It had become more difficult to stand, and he needed the extra room to clamber to his feet. He always slept on the side nearer the door, ostensibly as the defender against intruders and wild animals, but really because he would need to leave the tent more often than she during the night.

From the car trunk, he carried the travel bags one at a time and stashed them in the tent, hers on the farther side. He brought the sleeping bags one at a time. They had not been rolled up after their last use, and they splayed out like a snake-in-a-can as he tossed them through the open flap.

The wife returned. "The hosts said they'll come by this evening to get the number for the Senior Pass and take the money. They're right there in the site next to the vault toilet, so it's pretty clean. Still has that odor, but it's tolerable. It's a good thing we're—." She stopped talking when she saw the concern on his face. She doubted if he was bothered by anything she had said. "What's the matter, dear? You look disturbed."

He sat on the bench at the picnic table and leaned his elbows on the wood top. "Do I need to get the cooking gear out now?"

"Not unless you're hungry."

"I am."

She said, "I'll get the gear. You just sit there and rest a bit. You look tired."

"Not at all," he said pushing his hand against the tabletop to lift himself from the bench. He walked to the car and in three trips brought the stove, the ice chest, and the cardboard box filled with utensils and plates. He started to slide between the bench and the table.

The wife pretended to search the table. "Oh my, now where's the bread? Oh, sit tight. I can get it." She held out her hand, palm down, toward him.

He snapped at her, "No. No. I wish you'd quit saying that, like I'm too weak to do my part. You cook, I fetch. You know how we do things."

"Just bring the bag with the bread and chips if you would. There's some fried eggplant in the ice chest just waiting to be eaten."

"Why did I bring the stove then?"

"Because I'm going to use it sometime today. You always look ahead. I like that about you."

When he returned from the car, she offered him choices: "With or without tomatoes?" and, "Onions or not?" then, "Mustard, ketchup, or mayonnaise?" She said *mayonnaise* as if it rhymed with pez. She had studied French in high school, but retained only four words, *oui, non, voilà,* and *mayonnaise.*

After lunch, the wife put the used utensils in a plastic bag to clean later after supper. She collected the paper plates and towels and took them to the dumpster. The old man accompanied her to help open the heavy bear-proof lid. On the way, they stopped at the vault toilet.

He dreaded opening the door, but the assault on his nose was disturbing in an unanticipated way. The sharp smell of a disinfectant mixed with the formidable odor from the pit. Someone had left the lid open but the seat down. He did not lift the seat. When he had finished, he kicked the lid shut and rejoined his wife in the fresher air outside.

As they walked toward their campsite, he said, "It's almost time for me to go into Ketchum for my fly-fishing lesson."

She stopped in mid-step. "What?"

He stopped and turned toward her. "My fly-fishing lesson. Don't you remember my talking about it before we left?"

"No. You never mentioned it."

"Yes, I did. At least twice."

"Was I in the room?"

He hesitated as he tried to picture the event. "Probably. Why else would I think I told you?"

"Never mind that," she said. "Why fishing? We're vegetarians."

"It's not about eating. It's about manly activities and pitting yourself against the forces of nature. Don't you know who's buried down the road a piece?"

"What's so manly about hefting a fiberglass rod, tossing a fake fly that weighs a fraction of a fraction of an ounce, and hooking a fish that wouldn't even come up to your knee?"

"It's the mystique, the bragging rights, the ability to say the one true sentence, "I caught a fish.""

"You mean, 'I caused an innocent fish unnecessary pain, terror, and suffering.' Some mystique that is!"

"If you put it like that, it sounds less like Papa and more like de Sade."

"They were both royal pains."

"Are you telling me not to pursue this dream?"

"Ha!"

The old man turned and walked away, mumbling, "I hate it when she criticizes me for no reason."

The wife followed at a distance., muttering, "And even more when there *is* a reason."

Together they drove into Ketchum and parked. The old man told her he would be back at the car by 5:00. She wished him luck. She began strolling aimlessly down Main Street glancing in the store windows at items she had no intention of buying. When she reached Second Street East, she spied a bookstore less than a block away. She spent most of an hour browsing the sections devoted to local interest and local authors, none of whom she had ever heard of. She chose two books and decided to return to the car by way of Leadville Avenue. A charming café with an outdoor patio caught her fancy. She spent the remainder of the afternoon reading and sipping, first an espresso, then a series of herbal teas, with only a short break for the restroom.

She was ten minutes late returning to the car. The old man

was waiting for her.

"I've been waiting an hour," he snapped at her.

She looked at her watch. "I thought you said 5:00."

"I did."

"You're soaking wet."

With a snarl, he said, "Really? I hadn't noticed. Let's get back to the tent so I can change."

The wife offered to drive, but he insisted. She covered the driver's seat with two layers of towel.

As he turned on to Main Street, she asked, "What happened?"

"I don't want to talk about it."

She waited a minute, then asked, "Did you catch anything?"

"If you must know, I may have caught a cold."

She smiled out the passenger window and thought, 'I guess he'll need a different true sentence.'

A little too much in a hurry to get dry, he sped through an intersection and was pulled over by a police officer who seemed intent on processing the citation as slowly as a glacier melts.

At the campsite, the old man brought the box with the canned and dried food and the ice chest to the picnic table. The wife set about making supper while he took the opportunity to change into dry clothes in the tent.

They feasted on 'burgers' made exclusively from mashed black beans and lentils seasoned with *herbes de Provence* and topped with cheese, tomato slices, and lettuce leaves. Cauliflower and broccoli sautéed in olive oil completed the meal.

She disposed of the paper plates in a trash bag and washed the pan, cups, and utensils. Because the area was bear country, he stored the food box and ice chest in the trunk and then took the trash to the dumpster near the restroom. Back at the campsite, he grabbed a book to read from the car and the electric lantern and joined his wife at the table. She was already immersed in *While You Were Away*.

They had not spoken since leaving the town. He was unwilling to share the details of his adventure at and in the Big Wood River. She was unwilling to disrupt the calm by asking him for those details.

As twilight fell, she put down her book. "I better get the tent ready for sleeping."

He was about to turn on the lantern when she grabbed it and took it with her to the tent. She disappeared inside. Hardly a minute had passed when she stuck her head through the flaps.

"The air mattresses, could you bring them here? You forgot to get them out of the car."

He was surprised and doubtful because he had already emptied the trunk and backseat, but he went anyway to retrieve them. They were not in the car.

"Are you sure they're not in the tent?" he called across the campsite.

She yelled back, "Well, I'm right here looking and can't see them anywhere. Aren't they in the trunk?"

"Well, I'm right here looking and can't see them either. Did you check with the lantern on?"

"How blind does he think I am?" she muttered just loud enough to be heard. She searched holding the lantern by her side. "Not here," she announced in a confident voice.

He muttered too softly to be heard by anyone else, "Well, tarnation." He walked around the car and peered through each side window. He said loudly and irritably, "The air mattresses: where are they? I remember I got them out of the storage shed."

"That you did. I saw them myself, right next to the car when I got in."

"You didn't say anything?"

"Why would I? You were still packing the trunk."

"I didn't see them when we drove off so they must be here somewhere."

"Were you looking at the driveway? I was watching that cyclist swerving out of your way."

"Cyclist?"

"She's okay. She was stretching her finger last I saw her."

The old man walked to the tent, stuck his head through the flaps, and searched. "They're not here," he said.

"Are you sure?" she said sarcastically. "Maybe if you held the lantern you'd see better."

At first, he glared at her but saw her irritation instantly and converted his glare into a sweeping perusal of the interior.

She said, "Should we go into Ketchum and see if we can find some?"

"No. It'll be fine."

"But—"

"I'm not risking another ticket. I'm too close to losing my license."

"I could—"

"No." The volume, edge, and finality of his tone convinced the wife to stop offering help.

The feminine, singsong voice of the Campground Host called from the edge of camp. "Yoohoo! I'm here to collect the camp fee!"

The wife greeted her kindly as she came out of the tent. "Let me get my purse and I'll be right there." Then to her husband she said softly, "Do you want to get the Senior Pass?"

"Of course!" he shouted.

"And you might want to keep your voice down until she's gone."

"Of course," he grumbled less loudly.

The Host wrote the license plate number on her ledger, asked for and received the Pass, noted the number, returned the Pass, took eighteen dollars total for a two-night stay, and handed the wife a receipt. Looking a little uneasy, she said quietly to the wife, "You might want to keep it quieter if you don't mind. There's already been a complaint about the shouting." Reluctantly she added at a whisper, "Bite my tongue if I'm sticking my nose into places I shouldn't look, but that is one —"

The wife interrupted. "Don't say it."

"Just sayin'." The Host walked the loop road to the next camp.

The old man and his wife sat at the table and read by lantern light until past nine. The wife knew there were no blankets in the tent, but she knew she would be less stressed if she omitted mentioning it.

The night was cold. The thin floor of the tent provided no insulation, and the sleeping bags were designed for light summer use in much warmer climates. His jacket seemed to hold the cold close to his trunk. The distance from the floor to standing seemed immeasurably longer each time the old man had to leave the tent during the night. After the third visit to the restroom, he decided to sleep with his shoes on.

He found that the root he had earlier ignored was perfectly positioned in the middle of his back. It was longer and seemed wider than he recalled, and it had the mysterious power of relocation, always to be felt beneath him no matter where or how he twisted himself. As the night progressed, he grew stiffer, colder, crankier.

At dawn, he left the tent to visit the vault toilet. After shivering all the way there and back to the campsite, he decided to forgo further fitful sleep. He admitted to himself that hope for an hour of continuous rest was unrealistic, that he was aching in more places than when he had wrestled a jackhammer for a week, and that it would be idiotic to spend another night without the air mattresses and blankets.

He lit the propane camp stove and set a pot of water to boil.

He could wait for his wife to suggest they break camp and return home. Better to live to camp another day. But he knew full well that she would never suggest what might sound like criticism of his planning, endurance, or manliness.

He put a tablespoon of instant coffee in his mug and a teaspoonful in his wife's.

He decided to wait until midday to mention leaving if he still felt miserable.

He poured the simmering water into his mug. When it came to a boil, he filled her mug. He went to the tent, unzipped the flap, stuck his head through, and quietly said, "Are you awake?" Then he noticed she was standing, already dressed, and holding her toiletry bag.

"Is that coffee I smell? How thoughtful!" She came out and sat at the table. "Do you have another flyfishing lesson today?"

"No. The fish can swim in safety today."

"I was thinking an easy hike, perhaps up Murdock Creek or that flat trail along the river."

He walked slowly, deliberately to the car and brought back his shaving kit. His aches and stiffness were not lessening. "I was thinking we should go home, get the gear, and return in a couple weeks."

She smiled. "Let's have breakfast first."

He said, "And then, we'll break camp. Maybe we'll take a short stroll on the trail by the Big Wood River, sit on the bank, and recite platitudes about the passage of time."

"What a lovely morning it is."

"And I won't mention the nine dollars you threw away by paying for tonight's camping fee yesterday."

"I'm glad to hear it. What would you like for breakfast?"

"Do you think we'll have to replace the air mattresses?"

"I'm sure one of the neighbors took care of them, like Mrs. Jensen did the suitcase when we went to Spain."

The old man said, "Oatmeal. Another enigma explained.

MATTHEW STRAMOSKI

PIECES OF EIGHT

I sat quietly, marveling at Sister Mary Jonathum's demonstration on the blackboard of how to write the number eight. It looked even more complicated than the number two, which had baffled my hand for the first seventeen tries, yet she effortlessly drew it while explaining precisely how we too could gain the skill.

She insisted that we avoid an hourglass figure and drew one with facility. "Notice how the pinched middle can hardly hold the top steady. Imagine your head on such a scrawny neck!"

She warned us against stacking circles, and two lopsided loops took their places, one above the other, on the board. "Look how skinny they are. Who would want doughnuts like these? Not a soul!"

Two seats in front of me, Jimmy Ray Seifert offered a suggestion. "They look like those shiny things on angels' heads."

Sister Mary Jonathum smiled through her patient explanation. "They can't qualify as haloes because no one has two." She tossed the stub of her chalk in a graceful arc. It clanged into the trash can, ten feet away.

She chose a new piece of chalk. "If you follow my instructions precisely, I promise beauty and grace will follow." She turned her back to the class, pulled her black habit's right sleeve up to her elbow, and extended her arm so everyone could observe what she wrote. "See how this eight has one little piece where the end doesn't meet it exactly right. It's sticking up on the left like a kitten's ear." She provided the space in the top half of the figure with two dots and a short curve below them and then added a long squiggly line extending from the bottom half's right side. "The poor thing needs another ear. Is it lying flat on its head? Or was it lost in some terrible accident?" Her laughter flickered across the room as she turned her head, her face ensconced in a brilliantly white, starched coif and wimple.

Linda Townsend, the girl to my left, whimpered softly and knit her brows. "Oh!"

Sister Mary Jonathum beamed at her beneficently. "I'm sure there was no accident. That ear is timid and doesn't want to be seen. Just like mine!" She turned her back to us, pulled up her sleeve again, and obliterated the kitten.

She then invited us to pick up our pencils and follow her lead by writing our own eight in our tablets.

My pencil was as thick as my largest adult finger. Yet I could manage it better as a neophyte than now that I have become accustomed to slender mechanical pencils. I opened my tablet to the last page, the only one that had not been filled already. I was confident. I did not even have to bite my tongue in concentration. At the crucial turn in the center, I glanced at the board. Sister was moving her chalk slowly, deliberately, all the while describing the creation of the figure.

She turned, beamed from the interior of her wimple, and said, "Everyone, write a page of eights." She moved toward the far side of the room and walked down the aisle between the desks, pausing here and there to lean low and correct, refine, or encourage as needed. One student near the back of the room took considerable attention.

I finished the entire page of eights. I laid my fat pencil in the groove on the top of the desk. I surveyed my effort with a modicum of satisfaction. It was a good day.

The other students became restive. A murmur began. Sister Mary Jonathum stood up straight and spoke in a gently authoritative voice, undoubtedly unaware of the consequences of her simple request. "Everyone, if you've finished one page, do another." She bent again to help the other student.

Another page? This was my last one. I had been asked to do the impossible. There was only one solution. I burst into tears. Life as I knew it had ended forever. There was no salvation for me.

Sister Mary Jonathum was at my side. "What's wrong?"

I sobbed in despair. "No—more—paper."

"You have space between your eights. You can write between them."

I wept more fervently.

"You could—"

I wailed.

"Can anyone give Mark a page?"

Linda Townsend tore one sheet from the abundance in her tablet and handed it to me, gaining my lifelong gratitude with one small gesture.

When I arrived home, my mother handed me a new tablet. "What happened at school today?"

"Nothing."

"Your teacher called me."

"Oh." I took my new tablet to my room and placed it on my desk beside the birdcage.

MATTHEW STRAMOSKI

ROOFTOP SANTA

Santa sat on the roof and leaned on the chimney. The crest of the asbestos tiles, snug between his glutes, anchored him. His annual round was almost finished. One gift remained in his sack. It was for Mrs. Claus. Other than the traditional requirement for secrecy, there was now only one reason to worry or hurry: Mrs. Claus's tantrum if she didn't get her gift on time——scarier than the 1865 attack by a sextet of Southern Slay Belles. Cute but vicious.

It had been a hectic night, as every Christmas Eve had been since he assumed the role of gift-giver. Dasher and Comet had always been hard to restrain and synchronize with the others. Dasher was unpredictable and good for only short distances. Comet was forever asking the others to admire his tail. Cupid and Vixen constantly snuck off together. Dancer whirled and posed pretentiously, completely misunderstanding what *en pointe* meant. Donner insisted on wearing gaily colored robes with fancy trim and hats adorned with peacock feathers. He answered only when called "Doe-nay." And Blitzen needed to be sedated every four hours.

This year had been made more difficult because Rudolph had organized the Reindeer into a union. The breaks every other hour for water and feed, not to mention the bathroom stops, made progress slower than ever. The pauses, coupled with the increased demand by a surging population of spoiled kids and miserly parents, made a nearly perfect recipe for failure. To make up for lost time, he skipped the cookies and milk, tossed the gifts into a haphazard pile near the tree, and blew a kiss to the Mommies under the mistletoe.

Santa had known it was a mistake to hire Rudolph. That red nose, he was sure, resulted from repeatedly overindulging in Christmas spirits. He had arrived in midspring spouting a ludicrous story about losing his spot on an Iditarod team when his antlers accidentally pierced a husky. Mrs. Clause insisted he be given a chance, in spite of his emaciated body and blank, glassy eyes. She thought his nose was cute and, at worst, would make a nifty nightlight if she housebroke him.

The other Reindeer instantly recognized him for what he was, but Mrs. Claus wouldn't listen. Rudolph's behavior became increasingly obnoxious. In his rare and short flirtations with sobriety, he complained of headaches caused, he claimed, by little worms that could only be killed by drowning. Then he would sink into a sour swamp of whiskey. Before becoming comatose, he would charge at the Elves and make dirty brown snow in front of the mess hall. He would vomit anywhere he happened to be standing when the urge came up, twice in Santa's sleigh. During games, he would spit at the opponents and explain that he couldn't help it: he was part Llama. Rules meant nothing more to him than challenges to violate and evade. No wonder they shunned him! Even the eternally and irrationally cheerful Elves began to lay traps for him. Fortunately, they had only toy guns, rubber swords, and snare drums and did not understand how to use them.

Finally, Mrs. Claus laid down the law. She had been willing to look the other way when she heard the rumors about Rudolph stealing sugar from the Plum Fairies. She had not batted an eyelid when word came that he was dressing the Gnomes in tutus and posing them as if they were dancing with Barbie dolls, their noses in prurient positions. But Mrs. Claus could not continue to ignore his behavior when she discovered him pelting polar bears with her day-old macaroons. She smacked him so hard, his antlers fell off. She shook her finger in his face and shouted, "You'd better hit bottom before I start hitting *your* bottom."

He swore off liquor. At first, Santa jubilated: Rudolph was on the road to health! But instead, he became a bigger pain. Grumpy and grim wherever he went, he inflicted his abstinence on everyone. His attitude made his fellow reindeer feel as grimy as the mess hall's grease trap.

Mrs. Clause took Rudolph on a long retreat and introduced him to religion. Santa was pleased and hopeful until the Elves revealed that Rudolph's worship of Thor and Odin was founded on antler envy.

Then Rudolph found an elevated consciousness and embraced a Social Cause. Within the month, all the Reindeer, even the B-Team, had joined his Fraternal Organization of Overworked Transporters. Santa tried to shut the door on that, but the Reindeer stopped it with their F.O.O.T. Mrs. Claus tried to put their F.O.O.T. down, but they refused to toe the line.

Rudolph had gone from rake to ringleader in record time.

And now, early on Christmas morning, with dawn fast approaching, Santa sat on a roof like a roosting stork, waiting to see if Rudolph and his minions could convince Mrs. Clause to compromise on overtime.

He hadn't really wanted the job to begin with. He had been completely content with his life on the European continent. He made a good living from traveling with his carousel, helping the kids onto the reindeer, unicorn, and goat mannequins. Conscientious to a fault, he would spend extraordinary care to reassure the young mothers that the rides were safe, even inviting them to inspect his equipment in the utility shed. But Mrs. Claus, who was better at accusing than proving, had gotten tired of alleging his philandering. She searched until she found him a job that would keep him and his merry-go-round out of circulation. She felt isolation at the North Pole was the ideal solution.

The one night a year he was allowed to roam——thankfully without close supervision——he was saddled with such a long and tedious schedule of deliveries that he could hardly find the time for anything more than a quick rendezvous in Amsterdam. This year, the interruptions imposed by the Reindeer had squashed even that miniscule benefit.

"It's just as well," he said as if lying to himself out loud would make him feel better. "I'm feeling less attractive with every gram I gain."

Sitting snowbound at the North Pole, doing nothing more strenuous than listening to the reports of spying Elves and keeping a list of who had been naughty or nice while munching on cookies, caramels, and deep-fried pumpkin pancakes had caused him to pack on the pounds. And really, he asked himself, what child could possibly have done something naughty that could also be interesting? At best, it might rate two and a half stars on the disgusting scale, like squeezing toads. Most of the nice behavior, he suspected, was due more to fear of parental punishment than to hope for a trinket from a stranger. That a parent would even promise such a reward seemed problematic. As if goodness could be ingrained by fear or bribery! Even Mrs. Claus guffawed at the idea of a saintly child.

Santa smiled and twirled the tips of his moustache between his thumbs and index fingers as he recalled certain adults in Amsterdam who were experts at being naughtily nice. He halfheartedly wished he could feel guilty for spreading such pleasure.

He had to give credit to Mrs. Claus. She ran a tight shop and knew how to crack a whip without inflicting permanent damage. She kept production on schedule and prevented the Elves from stealing and selling supplies and toys on the black market. But even she was worried about where this union of Reindeer would lead. If the Elves caught on—. But that seemed unlikely since their little heads were chronically cheerful. They had a seemingly endless supply of upbeat songs to carry them through their long workdays. They could make *The Volga Boat Song* sound joyous. Their attitude seemed almost artificial. Santa sometimes suspected it was drug induced. He had always meant to ask Mrs. Clause if she were slipping cocaine into their cookies, but every time he approached the subject, she would distract him by playing with his ornaments.

He brushed aside the thought that Rudolph would try to organize the Elves. "That would be unlikely," Santa reassured himself. "Like me and the missus, the Reindeer look down on the Elves. I've heard Rudolph say they're no better than trained gibbons and we could easily replace them with mutant ants. I agree; very little training would be necessary."

Prancer had often joked openly about substituting naughty boys. At least Santa thought it was probably meant as a joke, although he could never be certain of Prancer's real intentions.

Santa spied the first hint of dawn and, with it, his sleigh approaching. "So, they're coming to take me away. Mrs. Claus must have agreed to overtime. Too bad," Santa thought, "I'd rather be in Amsterdam."

MATTHEW STRAMOSKI

WALKING WITH THE DOGS

Barbara suggested that I curtail my conversations with the neighborhood dogs. "The neighbors don't understand when you bark at their pets."

"If I wanted them to understand, I'd speak English."

"You know what I mean."

"But the dogs bark at me first. It would be rude not to answer."

"You're just encouraging them. They won't learn to ignore you unless you lead by example."

"I don't know if I can keep quiet that long."

"Pretend you're on a silent retreat."

The next time I walked the half block to check the mail, the yorkie who patrols the house across the street began to bark as soon as I opened my front door. It has scraggly grey-brown fur and a compulsion to confront everyone. As usual, it bounced to the edge of the sidewalk, yapped in bursts of bravery, and dared to claim the middle of the road as its own. Pausing every half minute or so, it glanced to the right and left, as if checking for flank attacks, then claimed another two feet of roadway, challenging me to contest his sovereignty.

I pushed out my lower lip, silently conceded his victory and withdrew in utter humiliation toward the mailboxes.

The two Labradors next door bounded out to greet me. The chocolate Lab is named Sheila; Lily, according to Barbara, is a blonde Lab, although to me she looks more like Vanilla. They have never been ones to speak, preferring to block my progress along the sidewalk until I have stroked their necks and backs to their satisfaction. They pushed their faces against my thighs and grinned with open maws up at me. Having verified that I was still acceptable, they rushed back behind the house.

I have never seen the dog who lives at the next house, but it greeted me today through the closed door with its usual enthusiasm. Only twice have I seen the woman who lives there. She has long brown hair, a slim, tall frame, and an angelic smile. Normally, I would have spent a rewarding three or four minutes conversing with the mysterious voice from beyond the door, but having given my promise, I forced myself to continue without responding. I bent my head forward and down in hopes the dog would think I had joined a monastic order and forgive my silence. Then it occurred to me that the dog, like me, couldn't see through the door and probably had no idea what I looked like.

The side yard of next house is surrounded by a tall, white, vinyl fence. The gate is not an exact fit, so I can see the resident rottweiler through the gaps. Always excited to see me, it throws itself repeatedly against the gate as it snarls and growls and barks in the ferociously cute way it has of asking for attention and respect. When I reach the midpoint of its section of sidewalk, the rotter races, barking the entire way, to the opposite side of the house, where it continues to demonstrate its mastery of protective posturing. My heart felt saddened to leave its attention unrequited.

The house behind the bank of mailboxes has a dog whose breed is an enigma to me. It is one of those tan and white creatures with perfect posture, poofy fur, perpetually erect ears, and a tail curled like a chambered nautilus. On the rare occasions when the woman who lives with it comes to the mailbox at the same time I do, it will bark like a snippy snob. I always bark back before greeting the woman, who has yet to answer me. On the edge of her grass is a discreet sign requesting that I refrain from allowing my dog to sully her lawn. If she ever answers me, I plan to point out that I don't own a dog.

I crossed the street toward the row of electric candy canes lining the opposite driveway. To the north stretches a trio of houses. The first has blue icicle lights dangling from the eaves; the next has topiary-style wire reindeer strung with red, blue, and green lights, guarding the front door; the third, where the road bends to the east, is decorated with garlands of lights and an inflated scene of Santa with his elves. The decorations remain lit until Memorial Day, even at three in the afternoon. I could easily steer by sight at night to the mailboxes if I wear my glasses. When I come home late, their festive brilliance reassures me that I am on the street where I live. I reluctantly turned away from the joyous display.

There are no dogs on that side of the street except the yorkie, which was why I chose to cross over rather than snub the neighbors' pets again.

Of course, the Labs raced across the street to greet me as if I had been absent for years on an expedition to distant dangers and had finally returned despite their fears. I bent to pet their heads, necks, backs. Sheila sat on my right foot and pressed her muzzle firmly against my thigh. In her mouth was a ripped tennis ball. Sweetly, Lily swiped against my other leg. An instant later, they sprinted home.

Across from my home, I was confronted again by the yapping yorkie. I understood it acted from an inflated sense of responsibility, that it was on a mission out of all proportion to its size. The time had come to move our relationship onto a new footing. I stood still, stared, kept silent, hoping it would telepathically perceive my mental image of a wagging tail. The yorkie seemed confused by this strange new behavior. It raised a paw, replaced it in the same spot, moved right, left, lowered its head, stepped forward, backward. It paused and looked around, repeated the ritual.

The front door of the house opened halfway, and the second child, the chubby boy with the Roy Orbison hairdo, called, "Kooky!"

I was still wondering if he was speaking to me when the yorkie dashed across the lawn and disappeared into the house.

I took my empty victory home and told Barbara, "It has been a terrible day. I don't think I can get the mail tomorrow."

YAK ATTACK

or,

A Dubious Battle

So, I stop at the convenience store, the one near my house, on the west side of town, just as I do every morning, to get a cup of coffee on my way to the tennis courts. I'm especially looking forward to the caffeine this morning because I'm scheduled to play with Reese in half an hour, a mixed doubles match against a couple of pigeons who've been married to each other for half their frigging lives. Those two love to tell you how much they adore each other, how they can't bear to be apart, not even for the time it takes to play a doubles match, it seems. They trot out that same old excuse every time I ask them why they don't get better partners. Anyway, forget about them.

Today, I've got to be on my toes. I've been working to get Reese on my side for a long time. She's played against me before, but I've seen that she treats you differently when she's on the same side of the net. I've seen how she leans in to listen to her partner before a crucial point. Leans in and smiles, nods her head, and lets her partner whisper right at her ear, close enough to lick. She's a fox, a real buttercup. So, I've got to be on top of my game; I don't want her to think I'm some sort of wimpy slasher, a chimpanzee with a racquet. Caffeine usually boosts my game, and if it doesn't make me blabber too much, I'll be that much closer to scoring. I know she wants me, because I see her smile whenever I make a killer return and scratch my back with my racquet; that makes my biceps flex and my delts look ripped.

Anyway, this morning, when I walk into the 24/7 Store, the clerk, same as always, says, "Morning, boss." He seems to think calling me "boss" is a show of respect. I just nod at him, ignore his ignorance, and turn down the first aisle on my way to the coffee.

Normally, I can make a beeline to the java, but this morning, blocking my way, standing at the magazine rack in front of the coffee station, is a pair of yaks. That surprises me because obviously yaks can't read and no one's there to read to them. I think, "What the hell?" But not out loud, like I sometimes do. That just gets me in trouble most of the time, like when I thought out loud across the table from Rita, my high school sweetie, about how fine it would be to suck on that waitress's nipples. I was just stating the obvious, but Rita told me to screw off and the old fartette at the next table called me a jackass. It doesn't take me long to learn a lesson: Keep your truth to yourself. But Rita overreacted and left me (even though I told her I liked the look of hers better). Anyway, this morning, instead of breaking my way through the barrier of hairy yak flesh, I just stop, look them over, and size up the situation before I act.

Normally, I just ignore these oddities; I'm an otter-floating-on-his-back kind of guy. Almost nothing bothers me. Take, for instance, the time when I saw the lady who lives on the corner across from me cursing and kicking her Shih-Tzu for no reason that I could see. All the while, it hunkered down on the ground, its tail under its butt, whimpering. I just walked on by without saying a word, just as any good citizen would. I'm not one to come between an owner and her beast. Besides, any dog that wears its hair pooffed up like that is just asking for a whomping. Even the cops, I think, would've walked on by. She wasn't kicking her husband, after all. Of course, that afternoon, when she tried to shoot the dog, she missed the first shot and put a hole in my mailbox. Her second shot caught the pooch in the haunch, and then she put four more into its tiny head. Blew that pooffed-up hair all to hell. I called the cops because I knew my insurance company would want a police report. They arrested her sitting on her front steps, the gun on the walk between her feet. Then they found her husband, dead on the back porch, his toupee hanging off to one side, a knife right in the middle of his back. No one could have seen that coming. But, she should have known better than to kill the dog. I could have told her that it's always a mistake to draw attention to yourself when you're committing a crime. To top it off (and this is the part that really gets my goat), the police report didn't even mention the bullet wound to my box, even though that was the complaint I filed. I had to buy a new one on my own.

Anyway, I've got to admit that I've never seen a yak before (not that I know of), but I can tell that these are yaks because I know what they should look like. They ought to look like their name, and these two look like yaks to me. They've got that stupid, bleary, weary-eyed look on their faces, as if they've been working all through the graveyard shift. But we all know that they're lazy cows who sleep from dusk to dawn, only waking up long enough to chew their cud or shake off a nightmare about tigers. These yaks just ignore me; they don't even wag their tails; they just block the aisle while staring at the garden magazines. They're wearing fur coats that droop all the way to the floor, on a summer morning, no less. I write it off, thinking that it might be a religious thing, like Orthodox Jews, but secretly I think these yaks really ought to get a haircut, at least for the summer. I mean, really, they must be sweating like hogs under all that fur. I know it's their business, not mine. What rankles me, though, is that the yaks are loitering, blocking the aisle, occupying space, separating me from the coffee.

After looking over the situation, I can say that this particular pair of yaks has no business blocking this aisle, pretending to read, pretending they're going to buy a magazine. What gets my goat, more than their pretense, more than their attempt to look sophisticated and educated, literate even—as if they were

Kono or Wamu or that other gorilla that could talk—is that I can't get past them to the coffee counter. Normally, it's a beeline from the door to the thermoses, but with these yaks in the way I'll have to walk all the way around, past the chips and wheat wafers in the next aisle just to get my frigging cup of coffee. They're forcing me out of my way. I'm trying not to take it personally, but it's a matter of principle.

I don't have a lot of one-on-one experience with yaks. I think I told you already, these two are the first I've seen. In spite of that hole in my education, I can see right away that they need to hear a firm voice or they won't take you seriously. Sometimes I just know these things. It's a gift. Of course, even a dodo might've figured it out, just from looking into their blank eyes. It's pretty obvious they're dim.

"Excuse me," I say as politely as I can without sounding like a total wimp, "but if you're not buying anything, would you mind moving aside?" I purposely talk louder than usual; after all, they have a bunch a fur clogging their ears. You've got to take handicaps into consideration, you know. I think there's a law about it, too.

The closer yak, the bigger one with the longer horns, looks at me out of one eye, but doesn't say anything; and he doesn't move either. Now it occurs to me that I don't know if yaks have voices or not. They just might be mutes, like giraffes. (Those cartoons lie.) All the same, he could nod, if only to show he heard me. It's clear to me now that I've been too polite, so I say louder, "Are you frigging deaf? I asked you to move!"

This is when I find out that yaks have voices, and rude ones at that. They sound more or less like sheep on steroids. But what really offends me is it assumes I can speak Yak. Well, even if I could speak Yak, this is America and the beast ought to at least try to speak English, and I tell him so in no uncertain terms.

"English. *Hhh*abla English, Senior, if you don't mind learning something for a change." This I say out loud and loud. There's no reason to be polite with these fur-inners. They weren't asked to come here, you know. At least, not by me. They just show up on the shore and act like they own the place, like they were shipped here by some divine edict, like it was their destiny. I'd like to double check *that* manifest.

"Let them be." It's the clerk from behind the counter yelling at me. I just ignore him. I've got a right to be here, and I'm a steady customer, not like these yaks that just show up out of the blue. That clerk needs to get his priorities straight.

The farther yak suddenly lurches to her side for no reason and bumps the closer yak who jerks backward and puts his butt up against the counter where the cream and sweeteners are. That should've been the end of it right there, but I decide to be magnanimous. After all, it's clear they're visitors and don't know the right way to behave, thinking their cute customs from back on the farm are good enough for an advanced, sophisticated place like America, counting on our hospitality to overlook their bumpkin ways. It's clear the little one, the lady yak, caused him to step back. It's not his fault she's hysterical. But the closer yak, like a lumbering ox, tries to turn, as if he wants to look behind himself, swinging his big ass in my direction, and I can see as it passes that a sugar packet is stuck to his left testicle.

How can I possibly sweeten my coffee now that I've see what he's done to the sugar? How many times has this happened this morning? They've been hanging here for god knows how long, and it's obvious they don't have a clue about hygiene. There's no way I can drink coffee flavored with yak ball sweat.

"That's just plain rude," I say, slow and clear and loud. I like to give fair warning.

I turn around, go outside, and fetch my racquet from the car. It's a Wilson, made of fiberglass, but it can do some real damage if you know how to wield it. As soon as I walk back in, the clerk pops around from behind the counter. He starts yelling, "Stop there, boss! Stop, boss!" He's making entirely too much racket for this early in the morning.

It looks like the yaks think they've gotten away with being impolite, because they're still blocking the aisle. They're not the first to underestimate the American spirit. It doesn't take me long to teach that bigger yak a lesson. A good forehand with top spin knocks his head back, I hear his neck snap, and he collapses in front of Sports Illustrated. I follow up with a backhand slice to the top of his skull right between his horns; it cracks, and blood and sweat go flying. The magazine rack, the floor, the condiments are all covered with red dots. I'm even madder now because they made me get blood on my clothes.

The other yak tries to move out of my way; clearly, she's a fast learner. Even if she was the one that made him back into the sweetener, the one that started it all, I decide to let her off with a mean stare and a sneer. But the aisle isn't big enough for her to get out of my way.

Before I can point out that she's still blocking the way, "What the hell?" yells the clerk, still not clear on the concept that he's supposed to help me, his best morning customer, clear the aisle.

"He stuck his butt up on the counter," I say, unable to keep a little disgust out of my voice, "so you're gonna have to clean up anyway."

It's clear the clerk isn't listening. He zips behind the counter, and the alarm starts screaming while I'm still speaking. I should have known: This clerk is as dumb as the dead yak. All these fur-inners take each other's side, you know.

The lady yak goes hysterical. It's bad enough that she's still blocking the aisle, but now she starts moving her horns left and right. She's making all sorts of noise. Even though I don't know much about yak mannerisms, I know a threat when I see one, and she's definitely threatening me. I reckon it's justifiable to take her out of the game too, so I do a straight forehand, a whap to the side of her head, the sweet spot right on her ear. My follow-through is flawless if a little broad from being riled up. She's knocked off balance and bumps the coffee counter, overturning and smashing the thermoses as she flails. I realize I'll have to make due with espresso, and that makes me madder still. She's looking groggy, but still on her feet. I take her down with a two-handed backhand strike from over my shoulder, straight to the skull, sharp and quick. She has this expression on her face as she drops to the floor, like she doesn't know what happened. Total surprise, just the way I like it on the court when I look like I'm out of the game and suddenly hit an overhead smash that makes their jaws pop open.

"Damn," I say. "My racquet's broken." I toss it aside. The clerk's got to clean up this mess anyway; may as well just leave it on the pile. I've got another in the Ram, so I don't really care. It was for a good cause.

I clamber on top of the bigger yak, feeling like the king of the mountain. Then I hop over the other one to the coffee counter, as agile as a mountain goat. Of course, what with blood, brain, and yak sweat splattered all over the place, I decide I'll take my espresso neat this morning. I head back to the counter, this time stepping over the yaks' heads and almost slipping on the blood slick. The clerk is cowering under the register as if I was some sort of ape threatening him. I put my drink on the counter and ask how much (as if I didn't know).

"Don't hurt me. I have a little girl. Two years old."

I'm thinking he probably calls her "Kitten," but I haven't got time to discuss it.

"Shut up, 'boss,' and ring me up." Then I remember the frigging donut, and I tell him, "Wait a sec."

I've already got blood and crap caked all over my shoes and splattered on my white shorts and shirt. It's going to be hard to impress Reese showing up with filthy clothes, but I haven't got time to go home and change. I decide to skip hopping over the corpses. I don't want to risk slipping and getting completely gory, so I take the long way around, past the baked chips and wheat wafers, and fetch myself a donut with chocolate sprinkles.

When I get back to the counter, the clerk, trembling and nervous as all hell, yells at me, "No charge. Free, boss."

"Ring it up. I'm not a thieving magpie."

"Two bucks, boss." His voice is shaky, even though he's shouting over the alarm. He must be thinking that I'm intolerant of fur-inners in general, but it was just the way those two yaks were acting that irritated me. I've got no beef with this particular Pakistani. At least he speaks English to me, even if it's with an accent. I see that he only charged me a nickel for the donut, but I pay up, like the polite customer I am, and head out the door. Sometimes these imports have trouble with American currency. It's not my fault, and it's not my job to teach him how to do his.

When I get to my Dodge Ram and open the door to the cab, I look back into the store. The wimpy clerk is sweating in the corner, arms crossed in front of his thin chest. When he sees me looking at him, he crouches down behind the counter, like a prairie dog zipping back into his hole. I think, 'That skunk's got a yellow stripe.'

"What a wimp," I mutter to myself, out loud since he's out of earshot. "I guess he's not even good enough to be a suicide bomber, so they sent him over here to defend yaks." I think I ought to go back in and teach him what happens to scaredy-cats, but I'm late, and I've only got one racquet left.

I'd wanted to get to the court before Reese, but I'm probably too late. I know she's warming up by now. Damn! I can just imagine that cute bottom twisting as she hits the ball out of bounds: Lots of top, but no top-spin.

I can hear sirens screaming like banshees as I pull out of the parking lot. My guess is that the cops'll just tell the clerk to clean up his own mess. I head south on West Street, east on Ironwood, and south again on Palm, sipping my espresso the whole way, listening to the Eagles wailing on the radio. I'm late, but I don't speed. Getting stopped would only make me later still. That's another lesson I learned the hard way.

When I get to the club, most of the parking spaces near the tennis courts are already taken. I have to park way off on the far side of the lot. "Just another thing," I sing to myself, "trying to keep me from my destiny." I imagine Reese swinging her racquet back, balancing with her left arm, looking like a ship's figurehead. My, oh, my, but I love mermaids.

I drop by the pro shop to find out what court I'm on. As soon as I open the door, there's a tinkle of little bells. Lizzy looks up, gets as wide-eyed as a doe, and starts backing away. The space behind the counter is only a couple feet wide, so she doesn't get far before her butt bumps the display case. I check the chart and find out that I'm on Court 10.

I smile at her and make small talk; women love that. "I'm a little late, I know, but I'm ready to play."

Lizzy can't seem to find a word to say to me, and I realize it's probably due to the blood on my clothes. It must have caught her off guard because, usually, I'm very neat. Today I'm a bit of a mess, you could say. I like Lizzy: She's got long blond hair and big brown eyes; she's just a bit overweight (unfortunate for a girl who's only twenty-two), but she's always smiling and pleasant to everybody, even the crabs. And she loves telling me about the trip she took to Cancun last winter. I must have heard it ten times, how she'd saved up for two years. She told me she got the belt of bells for the shop door because they sounded cheerful, and I told her it was a good choice because they were too cheap for anyone to bother stealing. It's kind of a boring story, actually, the way she tells it, but I listen anyway, because someday she's going to let me ring her bells. Until then, I make it more interesting by sneaking peeks down her blouse.

Anyway, since I like her, I say, just to reassure her, "Don't worry. I just got some yak on myself this morning at the C-store. Can you believe they were pretending to read?" And I head out the door, leaving her standing there with her mouth still open. After I've rung her up, I'm going to have to tell her that leaving her mouth open makes her look like a bumpkin, in a sexy sort of way, if you get my drift.

As I get to the first court, I look back and see she's making a phone call. Doves can't help cooing: They've got to share everything right away.

It's a walk to get to Court 10. I head up the center aisle, passing the odd numbered courts on the right and the evens on the left. The walkway's lined on each side with chain link fence and dark green screen, so only a couple of players notice me as I pass. They look puzzled and I think back to Lizzy looking all flustered because I'm a mess, so I wave to them and call out "Good morning," just to set them at ease, but they all react by looking disoriented. I've got to wear yak blood more often: It seems to be a great way to discombobulate the opponents.

At last, I can hear Reese talking up ahead on the left and pops that sound like somebody practicing a serve to my right. She's yacking up a storm, gabbling like a goose. Then I hear her telling someone, "Well, we may as well get started." I begin thinking that the group has gotten someone to sub for me, which would be unfortunate. I hate to throw my weight around, but I did arrange for this doubles match, and I'm going to play with Reese. I set my jaw, determined to insist that the sub has got to go.

But, as soon as I walk in the gate, I stop short. My jaw drops. I can't believe my eyes. Not because the old couple that's been married for the duration is sitting on the bench at court-side, holding their racquets in their laps, oh so prim. And not because right there in front of them, Reese is standing with one hand on her hip and the other holding her racquet. It's because, there, at her side, bigger than life, is a yak. And its head hair's pooffed up like a Shih-Tzu.

I can tell right away that this yak thinks he's got an impressive set of horns. The way he's standing there, gleaming-eyed and smirking, reeks of overconfidence. It doesn't take me long to figure out that he's got designs not only on taking over my game but also on snaking Reese. There's only one thing to do about that, and the quicker the strike, the better.

I pull the racquet out of the case, raise it over my shoulder, and charge straight for the yak, my jaw firmly set, teeth bared, and eyes glaring.

Reese sees me, screams, jumps back. That's all the warning the yak needs. He takes off running across the court, bellowing like a cow being slaughtered. Damn, he can run fast. I'm so focused on hacking at him that I'm caught off guard, as the old man, the one who always yokes up with his wife, trips me. Sprawling on the asphalt court, I lose my racquet and scrape my hands and arms. My nose is bleeding, and my knees feel a sharp pain, but I still let out a mighty war cry. Then I get the wind knocked out of me when the old man's wife sits on me. Damn, she's heavier than a mastodon.

I keep trying to tell them (in a squeaky voice because I can't breathe with that ton on my back) that they're letting the yak get away, but no one listens. They just keep telling me to save my breath, as if I had any.

When the cops finally get here, they get that bulk off my back and cuff me. It feels good to take a deep breath again.

One of the cops, the short one, as fat as a panda, reads me my rights while his partner checks out Reese. That one's tall and muscular, wearing those wraparound sunglasses that make it hard to tell where he's looking, but I know what's on his mind. I can tell by the way he stands that he thinks he looks sharp in that uniform. He's chatting her up, in a low voice. I can't make out what he's saying because of the noise from the fat parrot squawking about my rights.

I say, "What the hell do I need my rights for? It's just a yak. I didn't even get to hit him. You should be cuffing that old coot for tripping me. That's assault, isn't it? Reckless endangerment, at least."

The fat one keeps on going on about my rights, as if I'd never seen a cop show. I realize you can't interrupt a parrot. When he's done, he asks, "Did you stop by a 24/7 earlier this morning, Sir?"

My jaw drops again. "What? Is this about the donut? It's not my fault he charged me only a nickel."

"No, Sir. It's not about the donut."

"About the mess? Don't blame me if he's too lazy to do his job. I'm not going to clean it up for him." The cop just stares at me without blinking, his face set so it's impossible to read him. *This* one doesn't need wraparound shades. "I didn't break the coffee thermos, that's for sure. It was the yak that knocked it over."

"Why don't you tell us what transpired, Sir, if you don't mind, from the beginning?"

So, I tell them all about it, from the beginning, but when I get to how the yaks were blocking the aisle, the fat one interrupts me.

"Can you describe the yaks?"

I think, 'What the hell?' I say, "They looked like yaks." I shrug my shoulders, and feel the cuffs scrape my back and cut into my wrists. Then I go on with "what transpired."

I tell them almost everything. I make sure to include the parts about how the Pakistani didn't do his job keeping the aisle clear and how he mischarged me for the donut. He's just going to have to suffer the consequences when his boss finds out what a lousy clerk he is. But I leave out the part about Lizzy making personal calls on the job. After all, she's as cute as a finch and can't help singing.

Finally, I get to the part about how the pooffed-up scaredy-yak took off screaming across the court, big horns and all.

When I'm done, I ask the fat cop, "Now, what's the problem?"

He tells me matter-of-factly, "They must have been domesticated yaks; the wild ones are mute." Cops like to pretend they know everything. His partner nods silently, a tough look on his face, his eyes hidden behind his wraparounds. Give me a break.

I get the feeling they've got an agenda. Out loud and slowly, I say, "So, what's your point, *Officer*?"

It turns out that domesticated yaks have more rights than wild ones. Of course, the pig's gonna side with the yak. I know he's just enforcing the law; it's not really his fault. He's got a quota to fill, like any monkey on a rote job. Anyway, how was I to know? I don't walk around with the frigging criminal code in my shirt pocket. Sometimes I think lawyers make these things up as they go along, creating a new group of special interests so the buzzards can sue a corporation, get rich, and crow about it the rest of their lives, while poor little lambs like me get sheared, chopped, and fed to the wolves.

MATTHEW STRAMOSKI

HUNTING THE DRAGON

"**A**re you the Hunter Jonah?"

"If it pleases you, Sir Knight."

"That is not an answer."

"I hesitate to displease you."

"It would displease me only if you claim to be him but are not."

"But I could be less than you expect, Sir Knight, less than you desire, less than you need."

"Wouldn't you be the Hunter Jonah even if I found you wanting?"

"If you found me wanting, then I would be as I usually am: in need of necessities. I would simply be a simple man. From where I stand, it seems I have no choice but to be who I am, but your choices look more plentiful."

"Choice? I am who I am because I was born to be who I am, one chosen by the only One with a choice."

"Words well spoken, Sir."

"If I had not been directed to find you, I would slice off your insolent head. Are you or are you not the Hunter Jonah?"

"May I ask why you ask?"

"You may not." The Knight reflected as angled sunlight flashed across Jonah's face. "I choose to answer instead of slicing you into quarters. My liege, the Lord Nettelbarcq, commanded I come to the assistance of his serfs. It seems there is a dragon about, and that it needs to be killed."

"There is a dragon about. I don't know its needs, having neither seen nor tracked it. I know nothing useful. Is there some other way I may serve you? Do you seek shelter for the night, feed for your horse? In those matters, I am your willing, able servant."

"Only in those matters? Aren't you a loyal serf of my Lord in all matters? Is there any whim that I could ask in the Lord's name that you would deny me?"

"I must confess I am from birth a lowly freeman, uncommonly unworthy of the Lord's attention. However, I have willingly surrendered to Lord Nettelbarcq my gratitude and service whenever he has asked me."

"Humph," the Knight grunted. "I begin to doubt if you are the Hunter I hunt."

"If it's skill you seek, then I have no doubt that I'm not the one."

"Still, the taverner was certain; in fact, he said you're the only one; there's no other Hunter except the ones who hunt roaches or beer. He was quite definite. It took only one threat."

"Besides the word of the Lord Nettlebarcq, why do you believe you need a Hunter? You look like you could slay a dragon between dawn and Sunday Mass."

"Listen and learn, then assess and answer. I left my Lord's castle and went straightaway to consult the Oracle of Orion. He said I was to hunt for a Hunter who would show me a Seer who had seen the Hunter hunted unseen."

Jonah scratched his chin. "Was it the Seer or the Hunter of the hunted who was unseen?"

The Knight squinted. "Oracles explain nothing."

"Then why consult them?"

"I mean that they explain nothing they say they see."

The Hunter answered thoughtfully. "I see. They see deeply in ways that we can neither perceive nor fathom. I don't remember seeing a Seer seeing me being hunted, but I once felt hunted by something I couldn't see while I was hunting something I couldn't see either."

"Is it you, then?"

"How could I know, Sir Knight, something so hard to see? I'm just a simple Hunter, used to sighting singly along an arrow's shaft. But I can direct you to a Seer who might see the explanation well enough to show it to you."

"Aha! Then you *are* the Hunter who will show me the Seer. It has been foreseen; therefore you, Jonah the Hunter, must guide me to this Seer."

Jonah inhaled deeply and quickly. He closed his eyes, resigned himself to the unforeseen task, and exhaled. "It is my pleasure and privilege to escort you, Sir Knight, to the Seer who may have seen me unseen, the second of the second-sighted you are to see." Jonah held up his catch of the day. "May I first offer you a modest meal? It would be but scrawny scraps of squirrel, seasoned with prayers."

"As I am eager to see this quest through, I will feast only with my eyes, focused on the sight of the path before me, and be sated by the saw that the best meal is the one last seen."

Hoping that no meal seen soon would be the last, Jonah asked, "Sir Knight, it seems that you are embarked on a monumental quest. If some future chronicler should ask, what name shall I give?"

"Sir Metalmark d'Entrelacs."

"The Seer you seek is to the north." Without looking back, Jonah walked away from his home and family, hoping they were safe.

T wilight. The Hunter and Knight came to a meadow. On the far side stood a shack.

"That," said Jonah, "is the home of the Seer. We'll have to wait until morning."

"I will see him now. I haven't time to waste."

"He only sees people after breakfast."

"He'll see me now. I leave before breakfast."

The Knight led his horse across the meadow. His strides were long, sure, strong, and even; yet he remained in the same spot. Jonah watched him break a sweat. Jonah gathered wood and cleared a fire pit. As he skinned the scrawny squirrel, he heard the Knight panting. He roasted the scrawny squirrel, seasoned with prayers, while the Knight grimaced, leaned forward, struggling as if into a gale. The Knight finally stopped in exhaustion. When he regained his breath, he said, "I will wait until morning. This Seer probably works best with a belly full of fresh food."

The Hunter shared the scraps with the Knight, who then fell asleep in his armor on his back and began snoring at the stars.

In the morning, Jonah craved eggs so strongly that he thought he could smell and hear them frying behind him as he woke. When he rolled, he saw the Seer seeing to breakfast over a small but intense fire.

"Jonah! Good to see you again, although we've never met."

He had long gray hair pulled back over his ears and a short matching beard of uneven growth. Grey and white hairs peppered his black eyebrows. His eyes a fathomless black, his nose not large but prominent, and his mouth pulled pleasantly into a satisfied, closed-lipped smile, the Seer began to hum a single note occasionally embellished by its higher neighbor.

Jonah said, "I hope you see fit to share this breakfast you're making."

"With you and the Knight, of course. We couldn't leave him with a stomach as empty as his skull." The Seer shook his head. "All this way for riches, fame and a riddle. He deserves at least a bite for his efforts."

The Seer looked squarely at Jonah. "Jonah—in the belly of the whale—ha! What will happen if you remain in the belly?"

Thinking the Seer was teasing him, Jonah replied, "I would die slowly, in agony while the acid eats at me. It would be hard not to hate God every moment of the ordeal. I'd justifiably land in Hell for being understandably angry. But, of course, I'm not in a whale. That's just a silly tale, told in an old book my parents heard about second hand."

The Seer handed him a plate. "There may still be truth in it even if you don't see it. Many in the stomach of the creature that has swallowed their life are unaware. They wait and waste. Jonah, when you find what you do not seek, search in your heart for what you have lost. Ah, the Knight ends his night."

Slowly opening his eyes, the Knight leaned forward and stared vaguely toward the Seer, as if unaware of him.

"Good morning, Sir Metalmark," said the Seer. The Knight recoiled, startled by being addressed by someone he had not yet seen. The Seer laughed and said, "Allow me to introduce myself. I am the fourth you have sought, after the quest, the oracle, and the Hunter." He counted off the list with the index, middle and little fingers of his left hand. Jonah noted the Seer was missing the ring finger.

The Knight, finally able to see the Seer, looked over the short old man, clothed in grey and as scrawny as last night's squirrel. Scanning from the slippers to the loose cap, he smirked; the prophecy seemed to have played a trick on him.

"You have a question for me, which I will gladly answer, but please accept my unsophisticated offering for your breakfast." The Seer handed the Knight a plate of scrambled eggs and toasted barley bread.

"I want guidance, not food," said the Knight. "Are you the one to give it to me?"

"If you think not, then let the other oracle explain his own riddle."

"Then give me guidance so that I may be on my way without delay."

"I must eat before I work, and my visitors must eat before me."

"I must leave before breakfast."

"Then you are too late; breakfast is here whether you eat it or not. I counsel eating it."

Jonah said, "Quicker to eat than to argue."

The Knight downed the breakfast in four gulps. However, the Seer waited for Jonah to finish, then savored the eggs, lovingly and noisily masticated and swallowed his toasted barley bread, and reverentially sipped his tea. Jonah thought he saw a relationship between how swiftly the Knight ate his meal and how slowly the Seer ate his. The Hunter noticed the Knight became more irritated with each smack and slurp.

At last, the Seer sighed, waited for the last drop of tea to slide from his upturned cup, picked from the edge of his plate a stray bread crumb with the moistened tip of his index finger, stared appreciatively at the empty plate, then said, "Let neither your ambition nor your ego sway your understanding, Sir Knight. Listen well. The giver gets the given; the getter gives the gotten."

"Exactly what does that mean?" the Knight said.

The Seer cocked his head, as if puzzled. "I've heard that oracles explain nothing."

The Knight hissed, sneered, and said, "I don't see how it applies. Unless you mean I will give as good as I get. We're not exchanging gifts. I'm sure I'll give better than what I get and get other than what I give."

The Seer turned to Jonah. "You must take the path along the Dimwiddle until you meet the one with the points. Then turn up the next defile on your left. You will see your destination on the right. What looks dark from outside will be glowing inside."

"Thank you for all you have given us. May I know your name if a chronicler should ask for it?"

"Whatever for? Fame was invented so that artists can afford to create beauty. Some have distorted the idea in order to bring glory to their name and riches to their purse."

Sir Knight snorted, mounted his horse, and bid the Hunter to follow the path along the Dimwiddle. Sir d'Entrelacs turned to the Seer. "I will return to settle the bill for this paltry platitude once I have achieved my goal of greatness."

T he Hunter and the Knight angled across the meadow and found the head of a vague path that meandered through a grove of pines before emerging at a wide ford in the cold Dimwiddle River. They made their way along the suggestion of a path across a steep slope. Two days they followed the trail through alternating forest and glade, climbing ever higher and farther into the canyon.

At the end of the second day, from the forest edge, Jonah saw across a meadow, a few yards into the shadows opposite, a diminutive person sitting on a flat rock.

"Good day to you, sir," Jonah said cheerily.

"What?" said the Knight.

"I'm speaking to the one on the path ahead," whispered Jonah to the Knight.

"And good day to you, Hunter!" said the other, equally cheerfully.

"Oh," said the Knight, "there's someone there."

"Then you know me?" Jonah said.

"The famous Hunter, the son and grandson of Hunters! I've been waiting for you for two days. So good to see you at last."

The Knight pushed ahead of the Hunter. "Have you no greeting for me, knave?"

"Why would I?"

The Knight clenched his teeth, glared, drew his sword. "My blade will clarify my rank!"

Jonah said, "Do you remember, Sir Knight, that the Seer said we would meet the one with the points? Look and see: this one has pointed ears and a pointed nose, pointed fingers and pointed toes. He seems to be the one with the points. I bet he has much information to share. If you cut off his head, you will cut off the supply."

With his sword raised over his right shoulder, the Knight screamed at the stranger, "Speak! Or I will slice off your—arm."

Jonah moved to the side, far enough away, he thought, to avoid accidental injuries from a quest that wasn't his.

"I will pretend with you that I am responding to your

threat. But know that I was waiting and willing to divulge the information without intimidation. After all, I've been sitting here for two days. I'm more than ready to move along. Harken to my words." He seemed to point his tapered finger at the Knight, but Jonah thought it crooked toward him. "The leader leads the follower, then the follower leads the leader. But if the leader follows the follower, folly follows."

The Knight, plunging toward the weaponless stranger, rushed forward, swinging his sword in a mighty arc through the air, screaming, "No leader follows!"

Jonah fell to the grass and rolled away.

The stranger flew past them on the Knight's unarmed side as swiftly as a white-throated needletail and vanished down the path behind them.

The Knight heaped impotent curses on the pointed nose.

Jonah, now on his feet, said offhandedly, "It can't be far to the next defile on the left, the one the Seer told us to take. We'll make camp there and head up at daybreak."

They made camp near the right bank of the tributary to the Dimwiddle.

After a light meal of roots and herbs, Jonah drowned the campfire with Dimwiddle water. "Sir Knight, may I speak boldly and frankly with you?"

"Absolutely not. You forget your place."

"Never. Not even when I don't know what place I'm in. I'm here, as close to you as anybody else could possibly be at this moment, where an oracle predicted a Seer would place me, yet I wonder if this is my place or some random spot assigned by an intersection of misunderstood riddles."

"If you question divine oracles, then you question God Himself."

"I only question the veracity of some who say they are divinely inspired."

"There is no difference between questioning the integrity of divine representatives and doubting the divine."

"What if someone lied, claiming to be a prophet when

they were nothing more than an imposter?"

"Then God would strike him down in a heartbeat."

"Why then are there so many religions with so many divinely ordained prophets proclaiming the one and only god that no one else recognizes?"

"God's heart beats very slowly."

"Is that fair to those with shorter lives and quicker hearts?"

"God allows false prophets to test the discernment of the faithful. Some among the naïve are caught in the net. The trap was laid for others but the good must suffer with the bad. That's why the naïve fall under the special care of the clergy."

Jonah bid him good night, laid down, and turned his back to the Knight, who sat with his back to a stump. For several hours after falling asleep, the Knight proved his ancestry by producing noble gases.

In the morning, the Knight rose early and kicked the Hunter awake. "Destiny Day is here. We must leave now."

"Yes, of course, but perhaps it would be a good idea to bathe in the Dimwiddle before we meet the dragon. We smell like the devil's kin. The dragon might sniff out our presence before we are ready for him."

The Knight answered, "Our stench will not snuff our destiny."

Jonah drank a few handfuls of water and started silently up the steep defile. The Knight followed with his horse.

"We'll make faster progress without your horse. He won't be of any use in the dragon's cave."

The Knight reluctantly started to stake the horse near the Dimwiddle.

"There are wolves about. If he is free so he can run, he might survive."

At the first rest break, begrudgingly granted by the impatient Knight, Jonah asked, "I ask this out of curiosity, not from the slightest doubt of your destiny: What is the plan? And have you assigned me a place in it?"

"Ha! You suggest you could aid me? What could you contribute, standing beside me as if you were my equal? I will enter, inform the dragon that it is time to die, and kill him."

"My humble place then is outside?"

"You must enter with me."

"Arrows would be useless. I have heard that the scales of dragons are harder than granite. Only a consecrated blade in heroic hands could pierce them."

"You are afraid to face the foe."

"My father killed more animals than you and I have eaten. He said to always believe your foe is the stronger one. Wisdom isn't fear."

"Surely you've wished to slay a dragon. A side of dragon must weigh as much as a hundred bears. The harvest must have tempted you."

"A dragon's blood gives powers to those who taste it, but the flesh is poison."

"An old wives' tale. I've heard that buzzards who feasted on the flesh were transmogrified into falcons."

"Perhaps I will taste a little, just with my tongue, and become a swallow. But tell me, Sir Knight, what do you wish me to do in the dragon's den?"

"Observe. To sing my own praises would be ignoble. You will cower and whimper behind me so that later you can provide hints of my brave deeds to the troubadours. I don't expect you to be able to describe adequately my heroic deed, but the bards will add flesh to the bones of your account."

The Hunter blanched. "Must I go to the Lord with you?"

"Of course."

"You haven't the slightest doubt you will win?"

"None. My sword never fails."

"What if the dragon hears or smells us coming and fries us at the entrance?"

"My mother told me when I was four that a priest had told her when I was two that I would not burn before death. Everyone knows that dragons prefer to roast their prey alive. I cannot, therefore, believe that this dragon will kill me."

"Another oracle?"

"The testimonies of my saintly mother and a man of the sacred cloth—who could doubt?"

Jonah stood and started up the defile. Before he had walked three paces, he saw at the top of the rubble that sloped to his right a dark semicircle which appeared to be the opening of a cave. After thirty arduous minutes of scrambling over the scree, the Hunter and the Knight stood at the entrance and peered into the darkness.

Although Jonah had led the way, Sir Metalmark commanded him to stand aside. Jonah willingly obeyed. The Knight walked boldly into the grey opening. "Come, follow me," he commanded.

Jonah followed meekly. Thirty paces in, the tunnel curved to the left. Jonah saw that the cavern ahead glowed with an eerie, preternatural light. After another thirty paces, he stood close behind the Knight where the passage widened and heightened into a cavern.

"Wait here, Hunter, while I dispatch this creature. You'd only be in the way. Observe as closely as you can my skill, my bravery, my heroism. I will kill this villain solely for the sake of the weak farmers and merchants and thereby gain lasting glory. Kings and Popes will praise and reward me for this unselfish feat. My Lord Nettelbarcq will grant me the hand of maid Miriam. St. Peter will usher me to a place of honor. All because I risk my life to protect the weak and ordinary."

He stepped forward. The lidless eyes of the dragon turned toward his voice and the glow from within them caused the slope to shimmer.

The Knight whispered, "A hoard of golden coins, destined to be mine. They glisten from the dragon's wickedness. I will Christianize them."

Jonah watched the Knight step forward into the dim, weird light. As soon as his foot touched the edge of the pile of coins and gems, the light grew less muted and what appeared to be a worm as thick as the trunk of a mature ash tree rose up.

"Who? What? Why?" Each word was a puff of flame.

"Me. Death. Glory." The Knight's stride was clumsy, halting. He planted his weight; his foot sank into the coins and lurched him to the side and back. He shifted to his other foot; it slipped on the coins as if he climbed a sand dune. He leaned forward at an unsteady angle and steadied himself by leaning on his sword.

"Ah!" said the dragon. "You are the one the latest oracles spoke of. They did not mention the stench."

"If you know the oracles, then you know your destiny." The Knight lurched five paces closer.

"Better that you know your own destiny."

"Do not play word games with me, vile serpent. I will dispense with you as Daniel did with Bel." The Knight stumbled five paces nearer.

"I know neither Daniel nor Bel. Why ask the names of those I am about to kill? It's a waste of time. Who needs a litany of foolish losers?"

Another five paces, and the Knight was close enough to touch the dragon's front feet. "I would know your name so that the Chroniclers can rightly add it to the litany of my worthy foes."

"Ha!" The dragon reared its head and exhaled orange and yellow flames. They spread across the ceiling, heating the limestone until it glowed red and white. A fine dust of lime fogged the air and powdered the Knight. The Hunter, still at the entrance to the cavern, saw the flame form a transparent blue cone above the dragon's teeth, and between the fangs was the image of the Knight in his armor.

The dragon's scales spread open, revealing transparent skin over internal organs.

The Knight, his mouth grinning in amazement, sneered. "Meet your destiny, worm!"

He gripped his sword with both hands and thrust it into the dragon's neck above the collar bone and between the flared scales. It pierced the flesh easily, as if slicing jelly. He leaned and twisted to his left. A long gash spewed blood on his right shoulder. The dragon squealed. The Knight, knowing such a blow must be fatal, retracted his sword, held it dripping blood above his head, and triumphantly declared, "Victory is mine! I, Sir Metalmark d'Entrelacs, have given death to the vile worm!" He ripped off his helmet.

The dragon's neck reeled to its left. It belched flames as it swooped around in a wide arc until the head, over the torso, eyes down and neck up, stopped exhaling fire. It continued the circle, as if by reflex, back toward the Knight. Brandishing his sword in victory, he turned to face the Hunter and laughed at the look of fear on the commoner's face. The laughing Knight slowly and theatrically pointed the sword at the Hunter then brought the bloody sword toward his mouth to savor the death of his enemy and claim the powers of dragon's blood.

He did not see the dragon's head, mouth open, teeth bare, arcing toward him. In a single, smooth, sweeping pass it severed his head. The Knight's body, holding the sword, supported by the armor, stood rigid for an instant, as if uncertain what to do without its leader. From the stump of neck rhythmically spurted jets of blood. The body spasmed and collapsed chest down on the bed of coins.

The gash in the dragon's neck drew together, the bleeding stopped, the scales clinked over the scar, and its long neck and spiny head settled heavily on the hoard of treasure, the Knight's body under its chin. The dragon coughed up the noble head, ever so softly, a slimy ball of hair that rolled down the slope and settled in a dimple of coins, its eyes staring as if astonished and uncomprehending.

Jonah, unsure if the dragon was still alive, afraid for his life, struggled up the hill of coins and snatched up the sword. He was close enough now to hear the dragon's breath, and he saw the light in its eyes strengthen. Ready and eager to kill the dragon before it could recover and kill him, he straddled the neck and nestled the tip of the sword at the base of the skull between two scales where a swift thrust would sever the spinal cord. He prepared to lean his whole weight into the thrust.

At that very instant, he recalled the advice of the Seer, "When you find what you do not seek, search in your heart for what you have lost." One thrust would bring him the riches, fame, and powers sought by the Knight. But it was not the Hunter's quest.

He was a Hunter. His son would have been, too. A noble profession, but it was not his life. He hunted to support his family, not for glory, sport, or spite. If he knew another path, he would gladly walk it. The coins beneath the dragon's body would be blood money, gained through murder and theft, unfit for his wife, daughters, his—. His son! Long dead, long lost, long mourned! The plague didn't know sorrow or suffering. Death was what the plague did. To kill a dragon because a dragon behaves like a dragon? Would he kick a cat for catching a mouse?

The Hunter dropped the sword and slid as quietly and quickly as he could down the mound of coins toward the entrance of the cave. When he was at the foot of the hill of coins, the dragon lifted its head, eyed the Hunter warily, twisted its neck in a curious helix, and stood. The beast raised its head toward the ceiling, straightened its neck, and exhaled a stream of flames, lighting the cave with orange and yellow. Jonah turned, ready to defend himself although he had only his bow and a quiver of arrows on his back. The flame froze him in fear. Its center, the same transparent blue that heralded the Knight's death, this time held his own image.

When the flames stopped, the dragon extended its thick neck toward him. "Why are you sneaking away? What are you stealing?"

"I'm stealing away, but I'm not a thief."

"Empty your pockets."

"How do I empty the already empty?"

"Have you stuffed your quiver with coins and jewels?"

"Only with arrows, nothing of yours."

"Why are you empty handed?"

"Because I do not want to take your life."

"If you do not kill me, I will kill you."

"No need. I am a simple Hunter, also a husband and the father of two daughters and one dead son, but I don't kill except to help my family live."

The dragon crouched and leaned toward Jonah. "I know the prophecies: the commoner who leads the Knight, the unseeing Hunter of the unseen." The dragon twisted his neck to the right. "Prey or be prey: What is your choice?"

"If I kill you, you will return death, and then you will crouch in this cave craving your next victim. I had the chance to give you death, but I gave you mercy. The giver gets the given. I claim your mercy and ask you to spare my life."

"You cannot give life to me."

"Perhaps not. You already have life. That may be why I won't take it. I am returning home."

"Then I will roast you before you reach the outside. You must kill me, or you will never leave this cave."

"I won't follow folly, not yours, not his. While I led the Knight, it seemed his goal lead me, but I really followed my own: To return home by the circuitous route of ridding myself of the Knight's quest. Your lead is the same as his. You let him kill you so that you could follow his lead by killing him. As for myself. . ." Jonah choked on the words. He inhaled and held the breath before continuing. "I have given life to my children; now I must go and get life from them. For too long, I have lived in the belly of grief, focused on loss, overlooking my riches. I leave you the spoils of Sir Metalmark's armor and weapons. They would be useful in my trade, but I will not deprive you of what you have earned. I leave with as many arrows as I brought. My wealth lies in a tiny cottage near the edge of the forest. Kill me if you must but reflect first on the oracles. I do not want your death on my back," he said with sudden weariness, "for I have already brought too much premature death into the world."

The Hunter turned away. At the tunnel's curve, he heard the woosh of the dragon's fire, but Jonah did not look back.

MATTHEW STRAMOSKI

STILL LIFE: THREE BROTHERS WITH CHICKEN

I

The waitress distributed the plates laden with chicken, coleslaw, and mashed potatoes with gravy. "You boys just ask if you want more of the bottomless chicken. Enjoy."

Blain lifted his fork to dig into the coleslaw, but Marty held out his hand, palm down over the table, his sky-blue cuff rolled halfway to his elbow. "Wait a sec, Blain. Shouldn't we say grace first?"

Blain put his fork down. "If you must."

Paul asked, "Is it necessary? I mean, we're at a restaurant."

Marty said, "Isn't God everywhere?"

Blain shook his head. "Marty thinks God's keeping a ledger."

Marty laughed. "Well, isn't that what He does? Besides, it says somewhere, when two—or it might be three—are gathered together—"

Paul said, "That's to pray."

"And we're here in the name of chicken," said Blain. "Dead chicken. Murdered chicken."

"All the more reason to pray over them," said Paul.

Marty smiled indulgently. "For me, it's a spiritual practice. It doesn't feel right to eat without giving thanks for the food. Gratitude makes the meal sacred, and the food makes the gratitude sincere."

"Giving thanks for killing innocent birds," Blain said,

"doesn't seem right to me, but at any rate, you'll be covered on Judgement Day."

"When did you become vegetarian?" asked Paul.

Marty said as if reciting, "Heaven's gate has a miniscule lock opened by the punctilios of daily practice."

Paul exaggerated an eye-roll. "Mom would've said, 'Eye of the needle.' Much more poetic, though hardly original. Go ahead and say the magic words just in case the food is tainted."

Marty said, "I'm surprised at you, Paul. You're the family monk. I hope you haven't forgotten."

"How could you forget that?" Blain picked up his fork again.

"Leaf, root, gourd, grain and fruit, but nothing that ever walked, crawled or swam. It's hard to feel gratitude for a modest meal of cucumbers and cabbage. But it does make you capable of clearing the refectory quickly. Anyways, lead us in grace, Marty. I forget how." Paul made a sound resembling laughter, like "hee-hee," but it was less a word than a hint. Simultaneously, he dropped his head forward and to his left and shut his green eyes. When he opened them again, his bloodshot eyes reminded Marty of Christmas.

Marty loosened his navy-blue tie and unbuttoned his collar. He spread his arms to each side, his palms turned forward, like a pastor inviting his flock to share a sacred moment. With his hazel eyes shut, he cleared his throat and began in a voice that carried beyond the other brothers' comfort range. "Lord, thank you for bringing Paul to California to share this day with us, for providing him with an opportunity to reassess his life's direction, for leaving him an open option to return to the monastery which I hope he does, and for persuading Blain to join us so that we three brothers, who don't see each other often enough to realize and really appreciate what wonderful people we all can be--I mean, are--so we can spend too little time together. And thank you for allowing my wife and Blain's partner to see the wisdom of granting us some family time alone. I mean, in spite of her being family. And him, too, of course. I mean they're both

like family and wonderful people, too. What I mean, dear Lord
—"

"You're adrift, Marty," said Paul.

Marty opened his eyes. "I should have stuck to the script."

"You were never good at ad-libbing," said Blain.

Marty launched into a rapid-fire recitation, crescendoing as if it were a drumroll. "Bless us, O Lord, and these thy gifts which we are about to receive from thy bounty through Christ, our Lord. Amen."

To the relief of the other two, Marty made the sign of the cross and lowered his arms to the table. Blain scooped up a godly portion of coleslaw with his fork and balanced the pile into his mouth.

Marty thoroughly chewed and swallowed his first bite of chicken breast then said, "Do you remember how Mom used to make us take turns saying grace?" He stared at Blain as if waiting for a confession. "Well?"

Blain nodded.

Marty demanded, "Why don't you honor the tradition?"

Blain knew Marty felt obligated to press him lest this precious opportunity to bring him back to the fold be wasted. Blain tried to deflect the conversation. "I remember one time when I was in a phase where reading dramatically was my thing. My teacher accused me of 'overacting,' 'overreacting' or 'acting out,' depending on her mood. I felt I was thoughtful, passionate."

Paul said, "Yeah. It went on for about a year, though it seemed like two. It was hard not to criticize or groan or run away to a safe house. I figured you were trying to find your acting chops. But gracious me oh my, I was pleased as pecan pie when you finally moved on from *O Captain, My Captain*."

"Yeah. I was learning that one for school. Even Dad woke up long enough to tell me I was a bit over the top. I'd never heard the expression before, so I thought he was praising me, and I doubled down."

"I was ecstatic when you went back to silent reading."

Marty added, "I bet you still move your lips."

Blain continued, "Anyway, when Mom ordered me to say grace, I recited it with what I thought was devout attention, every word vested with importance, as if destined for God's own ear."

Paul made his laughter sound. "Does God really have an ear?"

"As soon as I finished, she slapped me down hard and fast. You know how she'd get when she suspected sin was hiding in your heart. Told me disrespect would not be tolerated, not in her house, not at her table. She sent me to my room right then and there."

Marty chuckled. "I remember it well. After you left, I told her I thought you'd put something real into it. I didn't get to eat either."

"Next time she told me it was my turn, I rattled it off like I was reciting the alphabet: fast and flat, ellemmennopee. She didn't say a word. No reproach. No praise. I got to eat that time. Lesson learned."

Paul asked, "And which ear were you talking into? The left or right?"

"I'd say the left. I don't know for sure if He has an ear, except in paintings; usually one. I think Michelangelo shows the left one." Blain paused to scoop up mashed potatoes with his fork. "Of course, I've never gotten an answer, so I can't tell you if it's real and deaf or just a metaphor, like those conceptions for the zoning board showing immaculate new buildings complete with trees, flowers, sunshine and happy white people pushing strollers."

Marty was incredulous. "Not one prayer ever? How do you know that? Maybe one was answered in a mysterious way."

"I judge by whether I got what I asked for."

"What in the world have you been asking for?"

"Nothing I ever got. Don't tell me the answer might've been no. I never prayed for rejection."

"But God's eager to grant prayers. It says so somewhere. In the Bible. It must've been you didn't ask for the right thing."

"Even my prayers have been answered," said Paul. "And once I heard an answer, too."

Blain said, "Not surprising. Isn't there a priority line, direct from the tabernacle in the monastery?"

Marty, who had just brought the breast to his lips, put his chicken down. "Really? What did He say?" He was astonished that God would have privileged a drunk with a personal message.

Paul said, "So, if He's got a voice, He probably has an ear, too."

Marty repeated his question.

"I'm not sure I should tell," answered Paul.

"What did He sound like?" asked Blain.

"Me and my big mouth." Paul took a mouthful of coleslaw and rolled his eyes toward the ceiling and then the parking lot.

"I'll tell you what happened to me way back when," said Marty, "and then you can tell us about yours."

Paul poked his coleslaw with his fork and gazed at it pensively. Blain thought he was looking for a sign, the way necromancers did in ancient times, and felt grateful that chicken entrails were disposed of far from the serving line.

II

Marty didn't wait for Paul's consent. "It was the day I turned twenty-two. I was at Fort Bragg. I had late-night duty, hustling and hauling heavy loads. When I got back to the barracks, I was exhausted. So, I showered, plopped myself down in the bed and closed my eyes." Marty paused, bit the chicken breast again and chewed with his mouth closed, his jaw moving side to side like a ruminating cow.

Blain remembered a similar tiring day in his Boot Camp: ten miles of double-time with a fifty-pound pack on his back and his M-16 at chest height throughout the march in atonement for a speck of dust on top of his locker. He plopped down on his bunk and closed his eyes. Immediately he dreamed of a huge skunk with ivory fangs attacking him. He jumped out of his bunk and knocked into Private Jansen. When Blain explained to him about the dream, Jansen decided the critter must have been Private Moore, who had not been seen in the shower for over a week.

Marty swallowed. "I felt a warmth wrap around me; light descend over me, and a cool breeze brushed my face. I heard a voice calling me over and over, gentle-like and from a distance. Stunned, I couldn't think, so I answered, 'Right here, Lord.' I felt like I was floating in the air, like a helium balloon, but not bloated. I was wrapped in love, wafting on my way to heaven. I said, 'Lord, I'm ready! Take me now!' But the Lord laughed. 'So much to do.'"

Marty bit off another chunk of chicken and chewed it deliberately. After he swallowed, he sipped his soda. The other two waited until he stuck his fork in the potatoes.

Blain said, "And—?"

Marty said matter-of-factly, "And then I fell asleep."

Paul said, "You went to sleep—just like that—without asking for details?"

Marty shrugged. "Yeah."

Paul put his fork down deliberately. "God speaks to you and in the middle of the conversation you fall asleep." The tone was at once scolding and incredulous.

"I'm sure He would've kept me awake if He'd had more to say."

Paul said through clenched teeth, "Well, I'll be cob-stoppered if—"

Blain interrupted. "How did it change your life?" He sipped his soda, trying to appear casual.

"Oh, I don't know. I didn't die or ascend into heaven, so I went back to work in the morning. It's not like I could've called Him up or sent a follow up memo. What would you have done?"

Paul said, "I guess I'd've got down to work."

Blain said, "I would've felt relief. By most accounts, those who hear God's voice are usually given a mission that ends in torture and death, or at least a bad case of boils and ulcers."

Paul made his laughing sound. "You've got to let go of those pious stories. They're not for our time, thanks to modern medicine."

"Wouldn't the story be the same for all ages?"

"It depends on who you ask. Intimidation, even the threat of Hell, is old hat. My opinion. Don't tell the Abbot."

Irritated, Marty interrupted. "What are you two talking about? I didn't say anything about Hell. God was reassuring me his plan included me."

"I don't doubt for a second that it came down exactly as you told us." Paul extracted a cigarette from his pack and resolutely tamped its filter against the tabletop. He noticed there were no ashtrays. "Can I smoke in here?"

Blain answered, "No."

Paul carefully returned the cigarette to the red and white pack, as Marty said, "Your turn. Cough up your story."

Paul scowled and opened his mouth then closed it resolutely.

III

Blain jumped in, hoping to defuse the situation. "I saw a TV documentary years ago. I forget the name, but it was about angels. Of course, they couldn't find a real angel to interview on the record, although they had a couple of crossdressers. Couldn't fly, but they could walk the talk as long as the people around them were pleasant. Neither of them thought good deeds were required, so they fit the role into their lives like it was summer stock. One had a foam star on a rubber stick. He traded in the wooden one after spending a night in jail for assault. Another wore wings on a harness around his chest and shoulders. He'd hoist himself up and dangle from the fire escape and preach to the pigeons. Anyway, there was this one alcoholic who—." Blain caught himself, wondering if the story might offend Paul. He sipped his soda then took another forkful of coleslaw. Marty studied his chicken's ribs now lying bare on his plate.

Paul invited, "Are you going to finish? Just pretend you didn't say the secret word."

Blain continued as if there had been no pause. "The guy came home late totally wasted. He said it took him a flea's lifetime to unlock the door. He finally stumbled into his living room, fell on his hands and knees, and vomited."

Marty grimaced. "We're eating."

Blain continued without pausing. "He tried to get up, but he collapsed, chest first into the puddle. He rolled over, covered in the stuff."

Marty's fork clattered on his dish. "Oh, good lord."

"He managed to sit up with the help of his coffee table, but he retched again into his lap. At that very moment, an angel appeared to him. 'You have been chosen by God!' The guy said he couldn't help but laugh out loud. How ridiculous that God would choose a vomit-drenched sot for anything but damnation."

"You're kidding—."

Blain, eyes glazed as if he were envisioning the event, ignored Marty's third attempt to interrupt. "The angel directed him, 'Help others,' then disappeared. The guy went to AA. He stayed sober and dedicated himself to working with addicts. It'd been almost thirty years. He couldn't say if it was really an angel or a delirium, but he didn't think it mattered because it changed his life."

Marty said, "Is that a true story?" He tried not to sound confrontational.

Blain realized he had offended Marty. "It's true that I heard it in a documentary. I don't know if it really happened."

Paul said, "It sounds like a fable. I like the one about the ape and the fox, or is it a gardener?"

Blain was happy to change the subject. "My favorite is The Goat and the Ass."

"Which do you identify with?" asked Paul.

"Right now, the frog," said Blain.

"How so?" asked Paul. "I didn't know there was one with a frog."

"Boys were throwing rocks at frogs in a pond. The frogs tried to hide under water, but the boys kept trying to pelt them. One of the frogs stuck his head out." Blain imitated a raspy bull-frog. "'What is play to you is death to us.'"

Paul said, "Made him an easy target, didn't it?"

Marty turned to Paul. "Weren't you going to tell us about your encounter?"

"You wanted to know what was said, but I don't think I want to share."

"I asked," said Blain, "what the voice sounded like. I don't recall ever hearing Him. Maybe you could tell that?"

Marty turned again to Paul. "Well?"

"It wasn't a sound from outside," said Paul, "not like the wind or thunder. It was like—"

Paul took another bite. Everyone was silent while he chewed. Marty took a deep, nasal breath to calm his impatience. Paul pulled a cigarette from the pack again, looked at it fondly, passed it under his nose, and inhaled its fragrance. "I'll be back soon."

Marty glared at the table. Paul stood outside the café window, facing the parked cars.

Blain said, "He doesn't want to tell. Let it drop."

"But we made a deal. I told, now he tells."

"He didn't agree."

"He didn't say no."

"He's saying no now." Blain stood up and limped to the restroom.

IV

Blain was back before Paul returned. They sat silent until Marty prompted Paul. "Tell us!"

Paul hesitated, his lips clenched into a thin, pale line. Finally, he let out an exasperated sigh. "I was fresh out of the Army—well, 'fresh' isn't the right word. I was about as pickled as you can get without shriveling. I went home and visited the folks for a week or so. I thought we were having a great time, but then Mom took me aside and told me, time to move along. I think—I know it was the boozing. I tried to hide it, but she got tired of clearing out the beer cans while I snored. Dad was there, but he didn't say a word. I took it she spoke for him."

"She usually did," said Marty.

"So, I took my old, beat up bug and drove off."

Blain interrupted. "You mean the one I bought from you for a hundred bucks, the one I gave to Martha?"

"That's the one."

"So that's what happened. Martha said someone stole it."

"I wasn't thinking about trivialities like ownership. I just needed right now to get away as fast and far as I could."

"Fast? That old bug couldn't speed in a school zone."

"Blain, please, let him talk," said Marty.

Paul said, "True. I could've outrun it barefoot in a sticker patch. But like the hare, I would've sat down every hundred yards for a cigarette and a nap. Anyways, I picked up some gear from Sears and drove 'til I got to Colorado. I had to buy I think it was four quarts of oil just to get out of Texas. We'd had a great time camping at Garfield Pass when we were kids, so I thought to head there. I couldn't even find the pass, much less the campground."

"Garfield. Something special happen there?" Blain usually remembered place names easily.

"That's where the bear tore our tent."

"Ah." It was Monarch Pass. He decided to tell Paul later, but forgot.

"So, I wandered around overnighting here or there, totally without direction, purpose, destination."

"Like Blain," said Marty.

"Then I spent a night in Rocky Mountain Park at Timber Creek."

Blain recalled being there on his last vacation before his divorce. Because his wife hated camping, he took his boyfriend who loved roughing it. Sandy went on a late-night stroll to the lake and later wrote a poem about it.

"—sitting on a rough rock watching the crick for hours, completely forgitt'n 'bout marauding bears—"

Blain wondered if he had confused the campground with another. Had Sandy walked to this creek? He'd written a poem about a stream, too, but Blain couldn't remember the details. Sandy wrote a poem a day.

Paul was still talking. "—my spit in the crick on its way to the Colorado and Pacific. I was thinking 'bout its journey from my front teeth to the tail of a whale way down south. I pictured it going all the way, making not a stitch of difference at all. It might've broke into forty-seven drops, but none of 'em would've mixed with the clean water. They'd've stayed on the surface, swirled like any ol' part of the river, but in the end, they'd've warshed into the Gulf, still apart. Not one grain of sand moved by my spit, no effect at all. So, I sat on the rock for—"

While Marty explored the extremities of his patience, Blain felt a sudden empty space between his lungs and above his heart. The scene of his brother John's death stirred from the mirk and rose too vividly.

The two brothers had hiked with the sisters Marylou and MaryJo the five miles from the trailhead to Clapton Lake. John sat on a rock near the shore. All the way, he'd been unable to keep his eyes off Marylou, had been flirting with her to the point of embarrassing Blain and MaryJo. Marylou had oohed in delight when John had found the cloven tracks of a whitetail deer. They had crouched beside each other. John had traced the edge of the two halves, making Marylou giggle by comparing them to devil's horns. "If it was a buck, you'd see his eyes right here." He leaned forward to indicate the spots, lost his balance, and tipped into her. She fell back, sprawled on the turf, and laughed as John avoided crushing her. As he helped her up, he stole a peck on her cheek. John held her hand longer than necessary and whispered to her. Blain could see her blush; she smiled with closed lips but did not pull away.

Where the trail widened in sight of the lake, Marylou had

skipped ahead to the shore. She reached down without bending her knees and wiggled her fingers in the water. John stared at her as he sat down on a rock. Immediately, he sprang up then smashed wildly with his walking stick at the ground. Blain saw the snake strike. John tripped, flailing backwards, and struck his head on a fallen log.

John's body lay gasping, choking, his eyes wide, his face bloated. Blain ran to help him, but he had no idea what to do beyond kneeling by his side. Marylou was crying and screaming. MaryJo shook her by the shoulders. John's swollen body froze. Was it only ten seconds? Ten minutes?

"—feeling totally lost and alone. And that's when it happened." Paul paused for a long moment.

At the table, Blain gasped and tried to shake the scene out of his head.

Toward the soft sound of Blain's exhalation, Paul peeked from the corner of his eye, then returned to watching his plate. He said, "I don't know if I should repeat exactly what was said. I was totally shocked." He hesitated again.

"You don't have to tell us," Blain whispered. "What's between you and God can stay there, where it's safe."

Head cocked to one side, the right half of his mouth in a feeble smile, one brow raised, Paul peered at him. "I didn't think you were lis'ning. So, the next morning I took my gear and drove to the only monastery I'd heard of. Twenty an' some years ago."

Marty asked, "What was His message? Something like, 'Get thee to a nunnery?'"

Blain said, "That would have been undoable, considering the Church's mania for sex segregation."

Paul shook his head. "I should have known better than to share. Besides, Marty, it would have been to a 'monkery.' But that wasn't it, anyways."

Marty said, "And to follow up with Blain's question, did this divine message make a difference in your life? I mean, more profound than a new mailing address?"

Paul laughed after his fashion. "Not a heck of a lot, no. It's been purdy comfy though. Sort of. The food's to be depended upon, but it's as bland as a new year's resolution. What's really nice is no one talks at the table."

"Are we ready for another round of chicken?" asked Blain. He wanted to divert attention to something he could more easily stomach than comparisons of epiphanies. The other two ignored him.

Marty said, "I'd say the change I felt strongest after hearing the Word is how I don't worry as much anymore. I thought you were asking, did I have a mission or want to dedicate myself to some preaching circuit. I doubt if that would be for me. I haven't got a gift for preaching. I think my clinic does enough good."

"You don't need to explain," said Paul. "But you're great at preaching, if you want my opinion."

V

"I think we should get another round of chicken." Blain was determined to change the subject, especially now that Marty had brought up his clinic. Blain did not want another oral tour of the facilities. Dialysis opened the door to too many insensitive and corny jokes.

"Well, I want to make sure you know it wasn't just some silly dream."

"I never thought it was."

Marty pushed his plate away and stood up. "I'm going to go ask for another piece of chicken. Who wants more?" Before anyone could answer, he sat down again and said vehemently, "Why do you two think you have to upstage me? That vomit story, that mystery message. Insulting! You may as well've just said you got the divine word, but it was written in invisible ink."

"That'd be a violation of the lemon law," said Paul. No one laughed. "Look, Marty. It wasn't my intention to upstage or downplay your experience. I'm sorry it sounded that way."

"And I was just spouting the only story I have that's on

topic," said Blain.

"You mean to tell me, Blain, that you've never had a spiritual moment yourself? You have to borrow yours from some stranger?"

Paul inhaled audibly, reached for his cigarettes, put one between his lips, and pulled his lighter out of his shirt pocket. He remembered the prohibition against smoking in a restaurant and jerked the cigarette from between his lips. "Why should he have one?" he said, pointing the filter at Marty. "There's no rule saying everyone has to have a mystic moment. That's why we've got priests, to tell us what we can't hear on our own. And scriptures, to make darn sure the interpretation's right."

"Did you hear that, Blain? Now you're being shut out of the dee-vine conversation. Some other fella's got to tell you what was said and what to think about it."

Blain said lightly, "I never put much stock in hearsay."

Paul said, "Sounds just like Mom, I know, telling us what we're s'pposed to think. I'm going outside to smoke. I could use another chicken breast."

Blain headed toward the restroom. He stopped by the counter on the way back and asked for a thigh. The woman cheerfully put the piece on a fresh plate and added more slaw. He looked at her nametag. "Thank you, Marilyn."

She said, "The special ends at two, so be sure to get more before."

Blain started to turn, but Marilyn said, "Can I ask? What happened to your leg?"

"I broke it running through the woods."

"Oh. I'm glad it wasn't something horrible, like a war injury or a car crash."

Blain smiled.

As he approached the table, he saw that Paul was watching through the window. The table had been bused, and Paul's place was devoid of food, plates, and utensils. Marty had another breast. Paul reentered the restaurant and, without glancing at the table, smiled at Blain as he passed on his way to the counter.

Blain put his plate down without commenting.

While Paul was ordering his chicken, Marty asked, "You're going to tell your story now?"

"What makes you think I've got a story?"

Marty looked steadily over his glasses and shook his head faintly. "Am I the only one with courage around here?"

Paul returned with a fresh chicken breast and noisily dropped his clean utensils on the tabletop. "Do we have to say grace again?"

Blain vetoed the idea. "People who are too grateful become annoying; they never get a second favor. Maybe we can demonstrate our gratitude instead of trumpeting it."

Marty scowled. "Mine was sincere and hearty, not trumpeted."

Paul sighed then made his laughter sound, his left fingertips pressed to his forehead. "Maybe we should switch to politics."

Blain said, peeling the brown, crispy crust off the thigh, "I didn't hear any voice so I didn't get any message, but I'll tell you about an experience I had way back when, just to complete the set. I was around ten, eleven. Not quite into puberty. My voice hadn't broken yet, so I at least sounded innocent. In real life, I had too many sins to count, but none good enough to brag about."

Blain scraped some of the flesh off the thigh bone with his teeth. After swallowing, instead of returning to the story he had promised them, he asked, "I was still wondering, the words you heard, inside your head, or like they came from outside? Was it an idea without words, more like a feeling? Exactly what?"

"What are you talking about?" Marty was irritated.

"The voices you two heard."

Marty said, "Oh. That. Huh. Like it came from above. I was laying on my back, you know." The irritation had left his voice. He was pleased Blain asked him.

Paul did not answer. He poked his pile of mashed potatoes with his fork and waited, hoping neither brother would press the topic.

"Well, so how did it seem to you?" said Marty while Blain checked the thigh bone for missed meat.

Paul sighed. The rush of air irritated his throat. He coughed and belatedly brought the back of his hand to his mouth. "It's hard to describe."

Blain stopped examining the thigh bone. "I've heard you can only imagine your own voice. But I think the person who told me that, as if it were a God-given fact, suffered from a poor imagination. I can hear symphonies in my head, and I'm not even a musician. Anyway, my point is, my question is, did the voice sound like yours or someone you recognized?"

Paul said, "Not my voice, and not one I'd heard. But I knew who it was. I had no doubt. Now, you started to tell us about some prepubescent experience. It's time to spill it."

"I'd almost forgotten." Blain dropped the thigh bone and looked toward the serving counter.

Marty leaned forward impatiently. "Well? Let me guess. Was it, dork, a smarmy knight?"

"Actually, it was a clear and starry night. The moon was waxing gibbous."

"Huh?"

Blain suppressed a smirk. "We were camping in Colorado. We'd finished supper and cleaned up the dishes and gotten the camp all set for the night when you, Marty, told Mom that you wanted to walk down to the lake. She told you to take someone with you, in case you ran into a bear, so you brought me along. If we had run into one, about all I could've done is bring the news back to camp that you were being mauled."

"What lake was this?" Marty asked.

"So, as we left camp, Mom told us not to go too far. We walked down to the lake shore and crouched and watched. I didn't hear you leave, but you did. I was just watching the water, the trees, the stars. Then, I felt like I was expanding, spreading out into space. Not getting thinner or dissipating, just becoming broader. I didn't have a sense of time, but it was a process that took place over time, so there was a sense of time passing without an awareness of time."

Paul grunted. Marty said, "I'll have to work that out later."

Blain continued as if unaware of the interruption. "Over the lake, above the forest, into the sky, moving out among the stars, losing boundaries, and feeling like I was dissolving, but without losing a sense of self, of coherence. Rather--it was more like finding out how completely everything in the universe permeates everything else, not separate, not absorbed. As if every cell in your body was equally aware of your totality. As if the edges of things were a figment, easily dissolved, easily reformed. At some moment, I'm not sure how far out I'd gone by then, I heard Marty say my name, and I was instantaneously and comfortably back in the body of a boy beside a lake. You asked me, Marty, what I was doing, and then you told me, without waiting for me to answer, that you'd been all the way to the opposite side of the lake and then got worried that I'd gotten lost or hurt. So, you came back checking the ground for my half-chewed body only to find me intact exactly where you'd left me. That's the whole story."

Marty asked, "But no voice?"

"Just yours. It came from outside and to my right because that's where you were."

Paul said, "Let me get this straight. Mom told you not to go far, but you took an interstellar trip. Is that right?"

"Most of the time I was a good little boy." Blain reached for his drink. "I wasn't disobeying, not like when I ran away from home. Of course, this was different because I didn't run. I just crouched in one place the entire time. And when I did run away, it was a conscious decision, although I didn't understand at the time what it meant to be homeless."

Marty said, "Like voting for water commissioner: a conscious, uninformed decision." He quickly added, "I'm joking, y'know."

Paul said, "You could say you ran the way colors run in the wash. Marty, were you disappointed he wasn't shredded by a bear?"

Blain refocused on his memory. "It started without warning. While it was happening, I didn't think about it. I lived it, without considering where, why, how. I wonder now what would've happened if you hadn't come back when you did. If there's a point of no return?"

Paul laughed. "I'm sure we'd've found your soulless body. Even if you weren't in it anymore, we would've treated it with the respect it deserves—maybe more—and then buried it before it could rot. My guess is we'd've dug a grave close by."

Marty said, "I recall Dad saying buying a casket and a cemetery plot was a waste of good money when all you really needed was a burlap sack and a shovel. I was worried about that when—" He left off midsentence.

"And Mom liked to hide family secrets, even within the family." Paul made his laughter sound and coughed.

Blain said, "*Especially* within the family. When I went for my driver's license, she told me not to worry about failing it. It wouldn't be the first time she'd have to come back. I had no idea anyone had failed."

Paul confessed that he took the driving part three times before he passed it. Marty said he passed the second time. Blain did not share that he passed on his first attempt.

Marty laughed, "I'm glad Dad didn't bury Mom in a burlap sack in the backyard. It's not even holy ground."

Blain said nothing. When he had visited the cemetery on the anniversary of his mother's burial, he had taken the time to find John's gravestone. It stood between one with a Star of David and another with a Star and Crescent. The neighbors' ages were twenty-two and twenty-seven. It resembled holy ground.

VI

Marty said, "I'm out of food. Who wants more?"

"I'd like a drumstick this time," Blain said.

Paul coaxed a cigarette from his pack, tamped it

on the table, and said, "Another breast for me." He went outside to smoke.

Marty muttered as he and Blain walked from the table, "I hope he doesn't expect me to fetch it for him." Blain decided to go with him to the counter. Marty smiled at the server and asked for another breast. He returned to the table.

Seeing it was a few minutes before two o'clock, Blain asked, "Marilyn, can I get a drumstick for myself and another breast for my brother?"

"Of course. I wondered if you were related. You look so much alike you could almost be twins."

Blain decided not to point out that Paul was six inches shorter and Marty four inches taller. He brought the plates to the table. Marty had left his plate on the table and was heading toward the restroom.

Blain saw Paul toss away half his cigarette. Back at the table, Paul said, "Blain, do you really think Mom thought dying in a mystical trance would have to be kept secret?"

"You're speculating about my death by the lake?" Blain's spine shivered and tensed for a second. "She wouldn't've known the cause, so she pro'bly would've feared Marty poisoned me. That's a secret most mothers would want to hide."

"Really now, you think she'd've believed he'd murder his own brother?"

"Pro'bly not, unless there was a hint of a reason to think so."

"What if you'd come back from the dead and told her the truth, told about dying of mystic melting, do you think she'd still've been ashamed of it?"

"Of course! First, she wouldn't take the word of a zombie. And she was always suspicious we were up to no good. Even when you'd do exactly what she wanted and double checked all ten commandments, she'd point out the detail that could've been a temptation to sin."

"I can still hear her asking, 'Where's Jesus in all this tom-foolery?'"

Blain noticed Marty at the counter. Marty gave Marilyn cash. Long ago, Blain had resolved to allow and never question Marty's charity.

"But merging with—" Paul stopped, unsure how to finish.

"If you're not going to die of old age, then nothing less than the rapture would've been acceptable. The hand of Jesus taking mine and drawing me into a disk of glaring light, up and over the clouds: the only way to go gracefully. And it would have to be public, so there'd be no doubt. Otherwise, my disappearance would be just another shameful blot on our reputation, and there was not a whit of difference in her mind between reputation and honor."

Marty sat down.

Paul said, "Even then, she'd want to grill the witnesses before announcing the triumph."

"And check with the parish priest to make sure it wasn't one of those Protestant abominations, like speaking with flaming tongues."

"Really, Blain, have you ever actually read The Bible?" asked Paul.

Marty said, "Doubt is in our genes. We learned early, find the problems in whatever we do. That's why I work twelve hours a day, why I have a successful business; why you," he pointed at Blain, "can't seem to keep a job for more than a year, and you," he pointed at Paul, "drink so much you've been sent away to think over if you really want to stay a monk."

Paul said, "Oh, let's not blame Mom for it all."

"Nope. We're all in our forties, so we're responsible."

Blain said, "The voice was right when it told you that you've got a lot to do in this world. It could've said that to either me or Paul, but neither of us would've done as much about it. And Paul—."

Paul said, "Blain, quit wasting our time pretending to encourage us. We don't need or want it."

Marty asked, "Are you going to let your life drift off into space, Blain, like your story, or are you going to hunker down and work at a career?"

"To thine own self be rude, and it must follow, as the mighty say, thou canst not be crude to any man." Blain looked at his drumstick. "I'm full. I can't eat this."

Paul and Marty both said, "Me too." Paul added, "Another chicken dies for nothing."

"I'll get doggy bags for us, so the sacrifice will not have been in vain." Marty stood up.

Paul said, "But you can't take food away from an all-you-can-eat."

"If we ask her nicely, she might give it to us."

"We can't ask her to break the rules," said Paul.

"I've already bribed her with a good tip."

"Good," said Paul. "I'd hate to have to be grateful."

While Marty and Paul boxed up the last pieces, Blain headed for the restroom.

Standing alone at the washbasin, he thought about the priest's eulogy for John. It dwelt on the futility of the path of sinfulness, on the betrayal by alcohol and the desires of the flesh, and on the hope of God's mercy. Hope was a last resort, he admitted, but more wonderful miracles had happened, so there was always hope. Yet the priest felt it imperative to remind all present that death comes even to those unprepared, and we cannot count on God's mercy.

Two months after the funeral, Blain had stood alone at his mother's bedside when she spoke her last words, a secret he hid in his heart. "What's heaven without my boy?"

Alone in the restroom, he rinsed his face with cold water.

MATTHEW STRAMOSKI

ADAM AFTER EDEN

I

S amuel plucked his harp as he sat on a plush puff of cloud in the far forty where Heaven's wall abuts Purgatory and lies tantalizingly close to Limbo. A Messenger Angel, Racheles, one of Gabriel's favorite subordinates, appeared before him in all her radiant glory.

"That's a new hairdo. Those curls are very becoming, but why blond?"

With a smirk she delivered a summons: "You are scheduled for a private audience with the Almighty in ten minutes."

"Can you tell me what it's about?" he asked.

"It would never occur to me to question the Almighty." She arched an eyebrow and tilted her head to the side. "Are you thinking about refusing? Don't you know it's dangerous to delay? Better early than punctual."

"I wondered if I needed to bring something. Like, for example, facts or a helpful attitude."

"Not sure, really. Something to do with those humans you used to herd." One corner of her mouth rose slightly. "You'd better scurry. You wouldn't want to add tardy to the list of your faults, even though it could hardly tarnish your reputation more than it already is."

Having often heard the whispers behind his back, the

distorted accounts of his own failure in Eden, Samuel thought, 'How the high love to gloat. Let one serpent into the Garden and they never let you forget it.'

II

Samuel, empty-handed and clueless, approached the Portal to the Presence. Michael stood, sword drawn, to the left, polishing his weapon as if preparing for inspection before sentinel duty. The edge burst into flames, startling Michael, and he held the blade out at arm's length. He noticed Samuel and said, "Well, it's about time. Did you take the long way around the Universe to get here?"

Before Samuel could answer, the Portal swung open, a gale swept him through it, and he landed prostrate on the cushy floor.

Said the Almighty, shaking his head, "Why are angels prone to fall face down when they blow in here?" He surveyed the floor between the Portal and Samuel's feet with infinite care and dizzying speed. "Could the floor be uneven? No, no. I don't see any tripping hazards."

Samuel said, meekly, turning his face enough to clear his lips from the clouds, "Maybe it's that little twist the wind does just before releasing me?"

The Almighty stared as if he were plumbing the depths of a paradox. Then he said, "When I created the entrance protocol, I rather liked the wrist flip at the end. Might I have overdone it?" He shook his head as if an annoying fly had landed on his nose. "No. Impossible."

The Almighty started to turn away but instead suddenly whirled and faced Samuel. "I asked you here," he said, "because

I have a project for you, one that is particularly suited to your experience. I want you to return to Earth to visit Adam. I've notified the Department of Transportation to expect you and revealed Adam's location."

"Is this a social call, or do I have a mission?"

"Both. Adam is close to death."

"But I have absolutely no experience with death."

"I understand that, but you know Adam better than anyone other than me. He will, I know, trust you enough to follow you."

"Follow me? Where should I lead him? Most of the time I'm not sure where *I* am."

"I want you to facilitate his passage, to lead him by the hand, if necessary, until he's safely through the Gates of Heaven. Lucifer has expressed a particular interest in reaping Adam's soul, and I want you to make sure he fails."

Samuel thought, 'Wouldn't the disposition of Adam's soul be decided by Adam?'

The Almighty answered Samuel's thought as if it were spoken. "I and *only* I am the one who decides who spends eternity where."

"Your command." Samuel said with as much of a bow as he could manage lying flat on his belly, "is my wish."

III

On a woven reed mat, Adam slept propped against the wall of his hutch, legs outstretched toward the entry. He wheezed softly, subtly, and shuddered intermittently as if with a fever. A commotion outside woke him, and the familiar, familial voices gained a sharp edge then suddenly scattered and weakened as they grew more distant.

"Aha!" Adam exclaimed when Samuel entered. "I wondered if I'd see you again. Make yourself at home." He managed a short laugh that ended in a coughing fit.

The angel sat cross-legged on the packed earth. "I seem to have caused quite a stir. Are those people outside your family?"

Adam's laugh was weak and breathy. "Most of them are family, but some are outside my family. They're all waiting for me to die. Ever so patiently! They quit singing two days ago about how sad they would to be if I died. Now they're hoping I'll hurry up and get it over with."

"Why don't they just leave?"

"They heard the Angel of Death was coming. Cain's great-great-great-great-granddaughter's great-great-great-granddaughter's son's niece fancies she's got the gift of foretelling. Seems she once predicted rain a week in advance. Hasn't gotten anything right since then unless you've got a new title."

"No. It's still Angel of the Lord."

"Too bad. They've been very brave waiting outside."

"Brave? They ran like water!"

"They thought you'd land inside and take me away through the roof in a cloud without seeing them. They draw lots twice a day to pick who peeks in on me."

"I think I was supposed to land by your side, but the Department of Transportation miscalculated and overshot by about thirty paces."

Samuel looked Adam over. The man had become emaciated; around his bald crown grew sparse white hair with a cowlick precisely in the center rear; his beard was long and ragged, spotted with tan grains. He wore a robe that was baggy, especially around the chest.

"You don't look well, Adam."

"I don't feel well, Samuel."

Suddenly, surprising himself, Samuel blurted, "I hadn't realized how much I missed you until this moment." He felt for the first time in his existence a moistening at the outer corners of his eyes and wondered what it could mean.

Adam managed a weak smile. "How long has it been?"

"Nine hundred twenty-nine years, two hundred forty days, five hours and seven minutes."

"Are you sure? It seems longer."

"It's eight minutes now."

"I see you still don't understand humor." Adam tried to adjust his position, gave up, and sank back against the wall. "Babies cry before they laugh, so maybe there's hope for you."

To Samuel, it seemed an odd hope that someone should cry, even if it led eventually to laughter. "Where's Eve?"

Adam furrowed his brows and quirked his head to the side. "You haven't heard? She died."

Samuel's mouth fell open. "No one told me. Not one word. I am so sorry." He wanted to ask of what, how, why. But he knew the ultimate answer would be the bite of the apple. He pushed into the pit of his mind a gnawing notion about the possibility of an unrevealed plan, the frequently recurring vague apprehension of some greater, more basic cause, perhaps incubating before Eve had been created.

Adam, hearing Samuel's discomfort, asked casually, "Have you been back to the old haunts?"

"Eden?"

"Of course."

"Was it haunted? I didn't notice."

Between wheezes, Adam said, "There were bats in the palms, but nothing more—." He had started to say 'sinister' but substituted, "Nothing spookier. Oh, and spiders that ate lentils."

"Is this an example of humor?"

"Not really. Just some theory started by the cousin of the great-great-grandaunt of that foreteller I told you about. I had explained to him that I got the vegetarian habit in the Garden. No one and nothing killed back then. He concluded the spiders must have lived on legumes, and lentils were the only ones small enough to fit in their jaws. Anyway, have you been back to

Eden?"

Because he did not want to give Adam another opportunity to discomfit him with humor, Samuel decided to avoid temporal precision. "I spent a couple hundred years watching the plants grow."

"Just you?"

"There was a Guardian at the gate, but she wasn't very talkative. No one replaced you and Eve, so it was a long, uneventful stretch. All the animals left. The sheep were the first to go, the rest were quick to follow."

"A Guard? Everyone knew we weren't coming back, didn't they? We knew we weren't welcome."

"I was told it was precautionary, not so much for you, but there was some fear about your descendants, not to mention the fallen angels who had escaped from the Fiery Pit."

Adam managed to chuckle without coughing. "Eve and I were astonished when we reached the second ridge and caught sight of a multitude camping out by the river. She said, 'Who are those guys? I thought we were the only ones.' They came in handier than we could have guessed once we had children to marry off."

Samuel said, "Even though there was great consternation among the angels that the demons would take over the Garden, not even one tried to break in. Technically, not even Lucifer trespassed. For the rest, evidently the two biggest treasures in Eden didn't interest them: they already had eternal life, and they were quite well informed about good and evil."

"You and the Guard: two bored angels in Paradise," said Adam. "Who would have guessed it would come to that?"

Samuel said with raised eyebrows, "Bored doesn't do it justice. The Guardian kept falling asleep. She'd drift off and interfere with the wind patterns. Raphael invented spiritual healing when she unthinkingly lowered her flaming sword and set her robe on fire.

"Eventually word came down to dismantle the walls and turn off the spring. The two treasure trees were uprooted. The

Jackfruit of Eternal Life was hoisted into Heaven, and the Apple of Good and Evil was tossed on a bonfire so as not to tempt the angels. I hadn't realized the fruit had become wormy; it was horrifying to hear them sizzle.

"It wasn't long before the rest of the plants died. Sofiel —I don't think you ever met her. You did? —Well, Sofiel was heartbroken. She kept sobbing and wailing, 'What do they have against weeds?' I didn't have a ready answer, at least not one she'd accept.

"Then Gabriel came with orders to demolish the walls. A couple trumpet blasts, and poof! Nothing but rubble."

IV

T he two were quiet for a long while. Adam drifted into sleep. Samuel waited until he woke then said, "I'm sorry I wasn't here when Eve died. I would have liked to see her again. She was spunky and sassy. She worried me at first, but in retrospect, she was refreshing."

Adam asked for water and pointed at a hollowed gourd beside the entry. Samuel brought it to him. Adam was too weak to lift it to his lips. The angel knelt beside him and steadied him with one hand on his back and the other tilting the gourd. When Adam leaned back against the wall, Samuel sat beside him again and asked, "Do you want to talk about Eve?"

Adam took a long, slow, audible breath through his nose. He looked away, frowning. He wondered if he should share, what to say, how to tell.

"What do you already know?" he asked.

"The last time I saw you two, you'd reached the crest of the hill east of Eden. I haven't heard a word until today, and that was just a command to come see you."

"Is that a good model for a father?"

Samuel was puzzled. "I'm not your father."

"I wasn't referring to you."

Now that he understood, Samuel decided not to answer.

"Eve," Adam said, "was never the same. Oh, she still had fortitude and grit, but the burden of guilt was hard for her to lay aside. She was convinced that I regretted going with her, that I would never be able to forgive her. And the curse didn't hint that atonement with the Almighty might be possible.

"Eve had already learned anger in the Garden, thanks to me and my fascination with gambling and sheep. Anger seems to be a natural emotion, even more basic and easily learned than love. In fact, a lot easier.

"We learned pain together. Eve—she was always the one to solve the big problems—she devised these coverings for our feet so we could walk across the rubble and hot sand. We'd lost a lot of blood before then. We grew cautious, preferring circumspection to spontaneity: 'Look before you step.'

"The animals refused to speak with us. I don't know the reason; they never told us. Some became belligerent. I don't have a clue what antagonized and alienated them. The sheep still flocked around me and tolerated Eve, but all the other animals ostracized her, even her best friend, Koko."

"I remember her!" Samuel smiled broadly. "A charming gorilla, yea high, beautiful dark eyes, and the cutest fangs outside a kitten. She was so friendly, but I could hardly get a word in edgewise."

"Eve's heart broke when she realized Koko wouldn't talk to her."

Samuel had been unaware how deep the rift had been between humans and animals. He said, "I would have found it hard to bear, too."

Adam whispered, "The animals began to fight among themselves. Eve blamed herself."

They sat silent for a few minutes.

Adam said, "There are dark places where an animal with a grudge can lurk before leaping. Eve became so afraid of snakes and dark places she unconsciously taught the fear to all our children. But" (Adam smiled contentedly) "the sheep stayed with us, even after—" (his eyes narrowed, the smile drooped, and a sob caught in his throat) "even after what Abel did."

His voice sounded dry. Samuel offered him a sip from the gourd. Adam's hands were still too weak to grip the gourd; the angel helped him hold it steady. Samuel recalled the first time he offered Adam a sip of water. It was in Eden, and Adam was as dry as dust. Samuel had had to caution Adam not to drink too fast or too much. How things had changed since then!

Adam smiled and continued. "If it weren't for Sofiel teaching us how to cultivate plants, we certainly would have starved. She helped us learn which plants were edible. Even some that we had enjoyed in Eden made us retch.

"Guilt, anger, pain, fear, hunger, sickness: We dreaded what the next lesson in evil would be."

V

A dam smiled. "Of course, it wasn't all hardship, or rather, not all the hardship was suffering. The more I worked with Eve to overcome the obstacles, the closer we became. There was no way we could have learned to appreciate each other so well, so deeply and completely, in Eden. At least, I never could have.

"Then Eve became pregnant. We had no idea what was going on until Sofiel explained. It seems that flowers do the same thing, but without ever meeting. 'Rather too chaste for my taste,' I told Sofiel, and Eve elbowed me in the ribs.

MATTHEW STRAMOSKI

"Eve was overjoyed: A little one that was both of us and neither of us! Night after night, I lay beside her, snuggling up to her back, wrapping my arm around the swelling roundness of her belly. It kept distending as if a melon was ripening inside her. I worried she would pop open like a seed pod. We got to be as jittery as a mouse cornered by a fox.

"Then the birth! I can't tell you how relieved I was when she underwent a controlled burst. We named the result—. Well, Eve picked the name: Cain. She said, 'We got what we got.' She said it was a pun. I still don't get it."

Adam's withered chest at that moment looked twice as broad, and his eyes flickered. "He was so cute! Eve said he looked just like me except the brown eyes were bright." Adam's chuckle quickly became a wheezing cough.

He went on when he regained his breath. "Another child, Abel, came about a year later. We thought we knew what to expect, but he cried nonstop for ninety days. Even worse, he cried for eighty-nine nights, too! Once in a while, he'd stop screaming and start giggling. We thought he might not be right in the head. Eve kidded me, 'He looks like me, but he takes after you.' At least, I think she was kidding."

Samuel said seriously, "It sounds like something she'd say as a joke, but I don't understand how insulting someone could be considered funny."

Adam said, "I guess you wouldn't. Cain was quiet, serious, diligent, always busy with some project. Abel preferred mischief, noise, tricks. He was always looking for the easy way and usually ended up with little or nothing to show for his lack of effort."

"All boys? So where did the crowd outside come from?"

"Oh, we didn't stop at two. The first four daughters arrived, one every other year. Eve insisted we name them after pretty flowers. I suggested my favorites: Thistle, Nettle, Butterbowl, Zinnia. Eve wouldn't compromise. They're Rose, Violet, Jasmine, Dahlia. For the next two, Eve asked me to name them after my favorite gemstones. Granite and Quartz were overruled in favor of Opal and Emerald. I was never good with names."

Adam drifted off for a while. When he woke, he asked, "Am I still talking? Where am I?"

"In your hutch."

He shook his head and chuckled. "I think I was about to tell you about the troubled times."

"Maybe you should rest and think peaceful thoughts. Better to conserve your strength."

"No, no, no! I've got to get it out of my chest. It's choking my heart. And who needs strength when you're dead?"

VI

A dam coughed and gasped. A few minutes passed before he could continue. "When Cain was old enough to do more than toss dust into the wind and call it 'dada,' he started to plant grain. He had a knack for it. It was delightful to see him crouch down to bury the seeds, make water and keep watch over them; he even sang to them. Did you know that he invented the planting stick?

"He was the picture of pride every harvest. He'd put a little grain apart every year. He'd heard me talk about angels and the Exiler, and he decided it would be a good idea to offer it in hopes that planting would be easier the next year, the rains more regular, the crows less greedy. Didn't seem to help much, but he kept at it. He was convinced it was important, and not in the sense of 'just in case,' but because he sincerely wanted to please the Exiler. I think there was a hidden desire to square things for his mother."

Adam paused, his head barely shaking, his eyes half-shut.

"Cain also saved some grain most years until he managed to put aside enough to convince a fallen angel to marry him. Of course, he had to sell off Jasmine to get enough gold to gild the deal, but it paid off well: Three sons and a second wife later, he was sitting pretty. In spite of the extra help, he still worked up a sweat every spring and autumn. The helpers usually ate more than they produced."

Adam tried to pick up the gourd, but it was too heavy despite being half empty. Samuel helped him lift it and held it to his lips while he sipped. He coughed and gasped, as if choking. "Sorry," he said when he could talk again, "it went down the wrong way."

The sun was close to the horizon now, and it shone in Adam's eyes. Samuel pulled the curtain across the entry and returned to sit by his side.

VII

A few minutes later, Adam continued. "Abel had a different talent. Like me, he preferred tending sheep. It's a simple task, well suited to the unambitious. You stand, you sit, you wave a stick, and you let the dog take the risks. And there are certain side benefits.

"I suggested from time to time that he do a little work for Cain to earn some grain to sacrifice.

"'Why?' he asked. 'Does he chew the grass for them?' Year after year Abel refused to acknowledge any outside help.

"One autumn evening, after Cain had cleansed his hands in a bowl of water and started the sacrificial fires, the Exiler came among us. He strolled around the place, not a nod in our direction, as if he owned the world. He walked right past Cain's offering without even sniffing the smoke. He wandered toward the pasture where Abel kept his flock, chatted with him, admired his ram, and commented on how contented the sheep looked. Then off he went in a puff and a wind.

"Abel was impressed. 'I've got to get me some of that stuff. Powerfully good way to travel.'

"Again, I suggested he try earning his sacrificial grain by working in Cain's field, but his own sweat did not appeal to him.

"The next time the Exiler sauntered past, Abel tried mightily hard to ingratiate himself, but other than a few comments about the size of his ram and a pat on the heads of a couple of lambs, no answer.

"The third visit was the charm. Abel asked him point blank how to get on his good side. 'I like a little smoke from and for food. If you lose a little more than is practical, even better. What's a little hunger going to hurt?'

"The next thing we knew, my favorite ewe, Baabette, was going up in smoke."

Samuel's jaw dropped open. He watched Adam's chest jerk as if he were sobbing softly, privately.

"I couldn't believe it! And Eve: stunned, bewildered, appalled. She wouldn't even swat a fly! It hadn't crossed our minds to kill an animal. We thought tending them meant taking care to make their lives as easy as possible. After all, we were put in charge of them! We thought for sure the Exiler would ferociously condemn what must have been an abomination to him."

Adam's voice became flat and hollow. "Instead, when he returned, he walked past Cain's altar without glancing at the ashes, went directly to Abel's, and inhaled. He stood before it a long time breathing deeply. I thought he was trying to control his anger, deciding what to do. I was afraid he was going to do something to Abel as irrational as what Abel had done to Baabette. But he said slowly, softly, 'Ah! Sweet.'

"Abel grinned and rubbed his hands together.

"As surprised as I was and as much as I hated what Abel had done to Baabette, I accepted the Almighty's judgment. Of course, I hoped that would be the end of it. The Exiler would deliver some magic power, Abel would be favored for a while, and Cain would go on raising grain. But the Exiler left in a flash of lightning without another word or gesture of appreciation.

"A dead sheep roasting on an altar: Abel standing beside it, arms akimbo. I was a good twenty paces off to his right, still stunned by what had happened. I could see his face. A change came over it, part curiosity, part craving. He walked up, inhaled deeply three times, tore off with his bare hands a chunk of Baabette, and ate her flesh.

"I vomited."

Adam's voice became sharp and tense. "Sacrificing a sheep became a weekly ritual, then every third day. Eve and I tried to talk him out of killing. We had always lived on fruit and nuts, leaves and grain, roots and mushrooms. We tried to convince him he was doing wrong, but he wouldn't stop. He was convinced that the magic had been withheld because more sacrifices were needed.

"Cain finally promised his mother to redeem him. They went over the ridge to talk privately. Abel never returned."

Adam coughed fitfully and then became silent. A long time passed before he spoke again. "The Exiler descended on a cloud. He examined the herd, asked Cain where Abel was, pretended he had nothing to do with anything. And then he went reflexively to his standard solution: send the supposed offender into exile."

Adam paused another long time. "We were suddenly burdened with caring for Cain's wives and children. Eve became pregnant again. She was a loving, caring, attentive mother and grandmother, but she was burdened with sorrow and the fear that she would lose more of her family. It was hard for her to open her heart again. She blamed the Exiler for causing trouble between Cain and Abel. And she blamed herself for bringing death and murder into the world. All she had wanted was a better life for us.

"We had another son, Seth. He was prolific. We were up to our knees in grandchildren. He built so many houses for them all it became a town."

Adam was fighting back tears. "But Eve could only see the losses, the empty spaces where Cain and Abel should have been. More than was good for her, she contemplated searching for Cain, but she didn't know which direction to go, how far away he was, what dangers lay between.

"Rumors, even legends, came to us about his feats: battles with giants, struggles with demons. None of the reports sounded like the Cain we knew. If true, then his heart had hardened. Eve took this, too, on her own shoulders. Not only had her one action caused her to lose her sons, but it also caused Cain to lose himself.

"Food was scarce and water scarcer. Our grandsons quarreled among themselves and then took cudgels to fight over who would get how much water and which fields to plant. They needed food so they took after Abel and began to slaughter animals and eat them.

"Then Rose died in childbirth. Eve laid down on her reed mat and refused every comforting word I could think of.

"Six months after that, Violet was gathering grapes when a wolf attacked her. She was severely maimed. Eve forced herself out of bed to help care for our daughter, but seven days later Violet died.

"Eve came home, laid down, tried to take some food but could hardly manage a sip of soup. She died still wondering how a single moment of aspiration could bring unending suffering."

VIII

Samuel sat with Adam for another hour before he asked, "Surely she set aside her resentment and guilt before she died? Surely she realized that the Almighty has a bigger plan for all of us?"

"What did she care? She'd lost two sons, two daughters. As she lay dying, she swore she would never ever, *never* set foot in the Almighty's presence again."

Samuel did not know if this refusal was feasible, but he hoped Eve would find a way to forgive. He asked, "You do know that you're going to die very soon, don't you? What's *your* plan?"

"I'll go, as I've always done, wherever Eve is, even if she's nowhere."

Samuel nodded, not surprised in the least. "Do you regret eating the apple? Do you ever wish you were back in Eden?"

"Paradise was a bore. Nothing but meaningless, unearned rewards without challenges. Lucifer promised knowledge, but we gained so much more: love, appreciation, compassion, intimacy. And the chance to be more than we thought possible. No. No regrets. I'd take the apple again without hesitating. I would even eat it first."

Samuel helped Adam sip water and watched him drift into sleep. The next morning, at sunrise, Adam breathed his last.

IX

S amuel did not attend Adam's funeral. Aware that his presence would cause fear and interfere with mourning, he left quietly a few moments after Adam's soul departed alone.

When Samuel arrived at the heavenly Gate, he stood patiently in line surrounded by Messenger and Guardian Angels idling away the wait with gossip and speculation. He paid little attention. When he finally came within sight of the Gate, he saw a sheep standing beside the Guardian-in-Charge. She looked bewildered.

Samuel asked, "What's this? Baabette?"

"Baa," answered the sheep.

"Still at the gate?" Samuel turned to the Guardian. "She's a sacrifice. Shouldn't she be let in right away?"

"She's got a pass, so do the rest of the sheep, but they refuse to enter without Adam. They were clogging the lane, so we put them out to the pasture in Limbo."

"Does Adam, do Adam and Eve have a pass, too?"

"Not likely, but let's see." The Guardian held up a list and perused it. "Here! Right at the top, 'Eve' and then just below it 'Adam.'"

Samuel looked puzzled. "They should already be here."

"Well, Eve got out of line as soon as she arrived and went off that way." He pointed in the direction of Limbo. "I think she was distracted by the bleating sheep. I haven't seen Adam yet."

Samuel turned to Baabette, crouched, and held her chin gently in his palm. "I'll take you to Adam, if you'd like."

"Baa." Samuel heard a tone of grateful agreement.

"This way," he said heading for Limbo.

AFTERWORD

Thank you for reading this collection of short stories. I hope you enjoyed it.

Reviews are helpful for other readers as well as for the author. Please take the time to leave a review on Amazon.com. It would be greatly appreciated.

If you would like to learn of new releases, please follow the author on Amazon.com or Goodreads.

Matthew Stramoski

ACKNOWLEDGEMENT

I wish to thank A. B. B.entley for her unfailing support and nearly infinite patience. Her suggestions and encouragement have been invaluable.

For several of these stories, my fellow authors, Kristina van Kirk and George Petit, have given invaluable advice, corrections, suggestions, and support as part of a critique group through the Palm Springs Writers Guild.

Seminars and classes offered through the Idaho Writers Guild have been excellent and inspirational, as well.

ABOUT THE AUTHOR

Matthew Stramoski

Matthew has spent his adult life in diverse careers. He defended democracy as a member of the United States Air Force, spending a considerable amount of time overseas. He then passed three years in various temporary jobs, from shovel operator to file clerk and receptionist. He has since worked as a bookkeeper, massage therapist, and spa manager. He earned undergraduate degrees in Music Composition and in Psychology from universities in California.

His most persistent interests are music, ancient and medieval history, literature, poetry, comparative religions, and languages. His favorite genres to read are mystery, fantasy, and science fiction. However, his eclectic tastes frequently lead him into other realms.

He is now retired, living peacefully in suburban Idaho with his long-time companion, Barbara, as well as three imaginary pets, two of which lack a clear awareness of boundaries.

BOOKS BY THIS AUTHOR

Lucifer Laughed

In this tell-all testament, Samuel, Angel of the Lord, rips open the secrets of heaven, revealing for the first time the truth about the fall of Satan, the seduction of Eve, the passion play, the origins of religions, and--most disturbing of all--the 'special' relationship between Lucifer and the Host of Angels. A gripping tale of sin and redemption from a most unholy perspective.

Selected Poems: On Subjects Sacred, Silly, And Serious

An eclectic collection of [poetry by the contemporary American author. The topics include relationships (dysfunctional and functional), religion, spirituality, political satire, and science. Included are 'Folded Time,' 'T-rumpasorass Psuedorex,' 'Lost at Sea,' and 'Visions.'

Made in the USA
Thornton, CO
05/21/23 19:02:32